D1191056

Strange Summer in Stratford

Strange Summer in Stratford

Norah A. Perez

Illustrated by Robert Ihrig

LITTLE, BROWN AND COMPANY
BOSTON TORONTO

LIBRARY OF CONGRESS CATALOG CARD NO. 68–21175

FIRST EDITION

Published simultaneously in Canada
by Little, Brown & Company (Canada) Limited

PRINTED IN THE UNITED STATES OF AMERICA

To Patrick, Matthew and Jonathan

Strange Summer in Stratford

1

SHAKESPEARE," read Jenny as their car passed a big sign by the side of the road. She groaned, tugged her hair, and made a horrible face. "As if I needed to be reminded. It's like having to take your medicine before it's even time."

Her mother laughed. Jenny could almost always make her mother laugh. "That's not a reminder. This Shakespeare is a place. A tiny village, in fact. And it's only a few miles from Stratford."

"A whole summer in Stratford," murmured Dr. McNamara. He was a rumpled man, with a pipe tucked snugly in the corner of his mouth. "How I'm looking forward to it."

"Well, I'm not!" Jenny leaned forward. "You know I hate the whole idea. If you'd really wanted to punish me you could have sent me to reform school or something."

"We considered it," he replied cheerfully. "But reform schools are so overcrowded these days."

"They're just full of disrespectful children," Mrs. McNamara put in.

"Then you should have sent me out to work. I could have scrubbed floors . . . or made beds."

"Well," admitted her mother pleasantly, "that occurred to us both. But considering the job you do around *our* house . . ." She paused tactfully.

"We just couldn't supply you with the proper references," finished Dr. McNamara.

"It's not funny!" Jenny wailed. She thrashed around in the back seat, trying to get her long legs into a comfortable position. There seemed to be so much more of her lately. "I'll be stuck in Stratford for months and months."

"Two," said her mother.

"With absolutely nothing to do."

Maggie McNamara heaved a small sigh. "Jenny," she said, "you always find something to do."

"Without one single, solitary friend."

"In two weeks," promised her father, "we'll be sweeping squadrons of children out of the house. You don't make friends — you recruit them. They never go home again."

"I will be miserable."

"Well, we won't be." Her mother was almost purring. "Your father will write his book about the modern Shakespearean theatre, and I shall just relax and enjoy Stratford. It's quite lovely, you know."

"I don't care! I'm tired of hearing about the Stratford Festival. I won't understand the plays — I don't want to see an opera — and I think ballet is stupid. This summer I was going to learn how to water ski."

"We've been over all this before," said her father mildly. "Next summer you'll learn how to water ski."

"I know a girl whose father sells orthopedic shoes," Jenny told him, "and he sends her to camp." She was thoughtful. "Why did you have to be a professor, Daddy?"

Her mother suggested with a smile that he hadn't been able to find honest employment anywhere else. But Dr. McNamara was suddenly serious.

"I am a little curious about something," he said.

"What, Bill?"

"There's something going on in Stratford that I don't understand. You know how helpful the theatre management was about my project at first."

"Yes — and now?"

"They've cooled off. I get the impression they're worried about something. Yet it's nothing I can really put my finger on."

Jenny's blue eyes were very bright. She leaned forward again. "You mean there's a mystery?"

"I'm not really sure."

"Maybe the actors are going on strike."

He laughed. "No, Jenny."

"Maybe the theatre is going out of business."

"No, Jenny."

"Maybe we'll be able to go to the cottage after all—I mean if they decide not to let you write your book."

This time her mother and father both spoke at the same time. "No, Jenny."

She flopped back against the seat. "I don't know what's so special about an old theatre anyway."

"Why don't you wait until you've had a look at it," suggested her father. "Then you can make up your mind."

They were leaving the rolling Ontario farmland behind them. Restaurants and motels began to appear on either side of the road. Jenny wished they were going to spend the summer in a glamorous hotel. She would wear dark glasses, sit beside a swimming pool, and call room service in the morning to order breakfast . . . chilled melon and French toast.

A boy about her age was staring out the back window of a station wagon ahead of them. As they pulled out to pass Jenny stuck her bare feet out of their car and wiggled her toes.

This time her mother didn't smile. "Stop that, Jennifer! Behave yourself."

Jenny moped, looking out. They were driving down the main street of Stratford. It was a city of color, a place of many flowers. Geraniums flamed in every household garden, and window boxes trailed a luxury of blooms everywhere she looked.

"We'll turn here at Queen Street," her father decided. "Then we'll drive around so that Jenny can have her first look at the theatre."

"Oh, I can wait," she protested. But the car had already made a right turn down a sunny side street. Many people were moving in the same direction. Jenny heard the clear and lovely call of trumpets.

"What's that?"

"It's almost time for the matinee to begin." Mrs. McNamara pointed. "Look!"

Jenny turned, and there was the Festival Theatre. It wasn't like any building she had ever seen before. It was a crown of sparkling glass, rich wood, and soft stone — polished by the late June sunshine. From the pointed roof, set against an intense blue sky, two gay flags stiffened in the breeze. Projecting from the building was a wide sweep of balcony on which three trumpeters were poised. A shiver traveled like a caterpillar down Jenny's spine. The sight and sound were incredibly thrilling.

All the people in their bright summer clothing were surging toward this spectacle with expectant faces. As the car curved down the hill, and circled around by the bank of the Avon River, Jenny glanced back and saw flower beds lying like open jewel cases all around the building.

Maybe she wouldn't like Stratford. Probably she would never understand the plays of William Shakespeare. But she had changed her mind about one thing. There was definitely something special about the Festival Theatre.

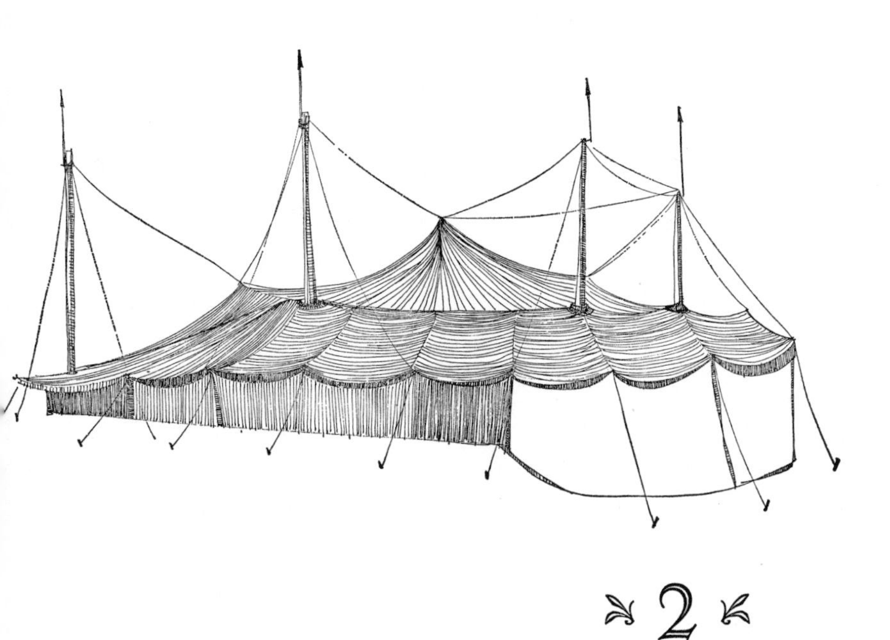

2

"AND WHAT are you planning to do today?" Mrs. McNamara's muffled voice came from inside a kitchen cupboard. They had rented an elderly apartment on Elizabeth Street, and were having trouble finding things.

"I don't know." Jenny gulped some orange juice, and took careful aim before spitting out a seed. It hit an ugly wall plaque which represented a bowl of hard glossy fruit. "Explore, I guess. What are you looking for?"

"The toaster. I had to send your father off without a decent breakfast."

"The refrigerator doesn't seem to be working

right," Jenny told her. "It made the most awful choking noises in the night."

"We'll have to tell Humphrey about it. Mrs. Dumphrie said he takes care of things for her."

They had met him the day before. He was the landlady's middle-aged son — a large soft fellow with a face like a shallow dish and two raisin eyes. Jenny thought he looked like an undercooked pudding.

"Where did Daddy go?"

"Over to the theatre." Her mother backed out of the bottom cupboard, followed by a tangle of electric appliance cords. Her face was flushed but triumphant. "I found it. I found the toaster."

Jenny, still in pajamas, cuddled her knees.

"Why did he go over there?"

"He wants to see some people and start his research."

"Does he know anybody?"

Mrs. McNamara blew on the toaster, dusted it off with a paper towel, and peered suspiciously into the metal nostrils.

"Oh yes. You know we've been coming here for years."

She popped in a slice of bread, and turned her attention to the battered gas range. "He wants a little more background on the young man whose dream was responsible for the whole idea of the Festival."

"Oh," Jenny said glumly. Is my toast ready yet?"

Mrs. McNamara shook her head. "I knew it wouldn't work. I just knew it. Nothing does."

"Try plugging it in," Jenny giggled. Her mother plugged in the cord.

"William Shakespeare was born in Stratford."

"Stratford-upon-Avon in England," Jenny said. "Everybody knows that."

"Well, this young journalist thought of having a simple Shakespearean festival right here in his home town because it had the same name. So many people became excited about his idea that in nineteen fifty-three . . ."

"That's before I was born!"

". . . the theatre opened. Your father and I were here for opening night. When Sir Alec Guinness came out on stage . . . well! I'll never forget the excitement in that tent."

"Tent?"

Her mother rattled the toaster. "Yes, it was a huge canvas tent over an open stage."

"What's an open stage?"

"Well, it kind of projects out into the audience so it is surrounded by spectators on three sides. The old Elizabethan theatres were built like that when Shakespeare's plays were being produced for the first time." She gave the toaster a final cuff with her fist. "Plug or no plug, it still won't work. You'll have to have bread and jelly, honey."

"But if it started out as a tent, why did they change it?"

Maggie McNamara sat down at the kitchen table, and her dark eyes shone.

"Because it worked!" She was emphatic. "The Stratford Festival was a great success. People kept coming back season after season, and donations came pouring in and made a permanent theatre possible. A man named Robert Fairfield designed the building you saw yesterday. It opened with *Hamlet* in nineteen fifty-seven, and it was one of the happiest nights in my whole memory."

Jenny was puzzled. "Why, Mother? Why would people come year after year just to see some old plays? Shakespeare died hundreds of years ago, didn't he?"

"Yes, but his plays live on. People come from all over the world out of a simple appreciation for his genius, and a genuine love for the beauty and profundity of his work." She laughed a little at herself. "I sound pompous, don't I? But it's true, Jenny. That's why your father and I come. Someday, perhaps, that is why you will come too."

A piece of jelly had stuck to the tip of Jenny's nose, and she crossed her eyes to watch it wobble.

"I'm going to be a skydiver, Mother," she said. "So, frankly, I just may not have time for it."

There was a noisy rapping on the door.

"I'll get it!" Jenny pulled on her robe and dashed

over to answer the knock. But the knob came off in her hand, and she dropped it on her bare foot. With a yelp, she grabbed the injured foot, hopping about on the other.

"Oh, my goodness!" gasped a husky voice from the other side. "Everywhere I go — calamity. *Calamity!*"

"It wasn't your fault." Mrs. McNamara had managed to open the door. "May we help you?"

"I'm looking for a friend of mine," replied a very small and very young woman. Her liquid voice seemed to travel from a deep well. She was dressed in a rough long gown that looked as if it had been made from an old burlap bag.

"You're staring at me," she accused Jenny. "You don't like my dress."

"Please close your mouth, Jenny. You *are* staring." Mrs. McNamara gave her daughter a warning poke.

Still standing on one foot, holding her throbbing toe, Jenny shook her head in dismay. "But I like your dress. I've just never seen one like it before," she protested.

"Of course you haven't." Their visitor threw out her arms. "Because I made it myself . . . from an old chicken-feed sack. Isn't it marvelous? Isn't it *me?*" She fetched up an astonishing laugh, and a long twisted braid of chestnut hair spilled down across the front of her dress. Dramatically she tossed it back over her shoulder.

"Stare at me all you like. I love to be stared at." Now her voice plunged in thrilling confidence. "Do you think I want to go through life without anyone remembering who I am? Of course not! I was born to be stared at."

"You are very beautiful," Jenny breathed. "Are you an actress?"

"An actress!" The reply was contemptuous. "I am a singer . . . a magnificent singer. I am Sybilla."

"And I'm Maggie McNamara," said Jenny's mother. "This is my daughter, Jennifer."

"Then I *do* have the wrong apartment. I am looking for Dylan Forde, the great Shakespearean actor. I have bothered you for nothing."

"It's quite all right. I believe your friend lives in the next apartment . . . just down the hall."

"Thank you," said the young woman. "Forgive Sybilla for intruding. Come to the Fare Thee Well some night and I will sing for you. Then you will forgive and love me."

"We'd like that," Mrs. McNamara said.

"Now I will go and surprise Dylan."

"I bet you will," Jenny agreed.

"Oh — here is your morning newspaper." Sybilla pulled it out from a hidden pocket in her strange garment. "I was going to borrow it. Not to read, of course. I never read newspapers."

"What do you do with them?" Jenny asked.

"I make jewelry. Beautiful jewelry. I will make you some fantastic earrings."

Mrs. McNamara said hastily, "Jenny is only thirteen. She's very tall for her age."

But Sybilla was pointing to the front page. "No, I don't usually read newspapers, but today . . . how can one avoid such shocking reports?" She gave a deep shudder. Her green-lidded eyes were tragic.

FIRE DAMAGE SLIGHT read the headline. The story underneath said that the fire which had been discovered blazing in the men's washroom of the Festival Theatre had been extinguished before any extensive damage was done.

" 'Police are investigating the possibility of arson,' " Sybilla read. "Hah! They should be."

3

THE DAY was shining when Jenny set out on her first exploration of the city of Stratford. Overhead the sky was a deep blue lake — the racing clouds like giddy sailboats. Just before she reached the downtown business section, a Lions Club pool glittered in the morning sunshine. If she could go swimming, things might not be such a bore after all. Once across the bridge, she stopped to decide which direction to take. To her right was the thatched entrance to a little park. Her mother had often mentioned the Shakespearean Gardens. Far to her left, past the municipal parking lot and the white geometric shapes of a small dam, she caught the quiet glimmer of Victoria Lake. On it the small paddlewheel boats made flashes of color. Canoes, like bright minnows, were darting in the direction of the Festival Theatre. She decided to go and have a look at them.

At the edge of the water were tables and chairs under gay fringed beach umbrellas. On the dam were some girls about her own age. They were jumping into the water with all their clothes on. Jenny knew that her mother would have some firm opinions about that.

She sat down and watched a young couple climb into one of the paddlewheels. The Festival symbol, a broad S with the head of a swan and two thick horizontal bars for the tail, was painted on the side of the boat. The boy and girl were skinny and serious-looking. He wore a spring growth of whiskers on his chin and she carried a heavy book under her arm. Sitting in the stern, the boy began to work the wooden levers that turned the wheel. While they moved out into the lake the girl opened her book. Her fresh voice carried clearly across the water.

"*Make me a willow cabin at your gate,*
And call upon my soul within the house;
Write loyal cantons of contemned love
And sing them loud even in the dead of night;"

Jenny didn't understand a word of it, but she thought it sounded rather nice.

"*Halloo your name to the reverberate hills,*
And make the babbling gossip of the air
Cry out 'Olivia!' "

The name Olivia was mockingly repeated by a voice behind her. Turning quickly, she met the smiling eyes of a boy who was also watching the lovers' departure.

"Olivia," he repeated, clasping his hands romantically. "I have a sister Olivia. But she has freckles all over."

Jenny stared at him.

"I know you," he told her. "You waved at me yesterday."

"I didn't wave at anybody yesterday," she contradicted him. "I was mad at the whole wide world."

"You waved your foot."

"Oh." She grinned. "Were you the boy in the station wagon?"

"I was."

"What is that girl reading?"

"It's part of Viola's speech from *Twelfth Night.* I have a sister Viola too."

"*Twelfth Night?*"

"Yes. That's a comedy by William Shakespeare."

He was a slim boy with a thin face and dark alert eyes. "How about going for a boat ride?"

"I'd better not."

"Are you going to be in Stratford for long?"

"Too long." She gave a despairing sigh. "The whole summer, that's how long."

"Cheer up," he said. "So am I. It's not so bad."

"You mean you like it here?"

"Yes, I like it here. I work here."

She studied him silently.

"I'm an actor," he explained.

Jenny was skeptical. "You're just a boy," she replied. "Boys can't be actors."

"Why not? In Shakespeare's day, boys were very good actors. They got to play all the female parts because ladies weren't allowed on the stage at all. What do you think of that?"

"I think women didn't know when they were well off!"

"You don't like actresses?"

"I don't happen to know any," she admitted. "Or actors, either. But I guess they're a pretty strange bunch."

"Why do you say that?"

"Oh, the things you see in the paper, for instance. They get married a lot of times, and the men never cut their hair."

He laughed. "Wait until you meet my father. He's one of the principal players here, and his name is Alexander Cardiff.

"I'm Toby."

"Jenny's my name. Jenny McNamara." She smiled at him, and they fell into step as they began to walk in the direction of Ontario Street. "Are you really an actor? You don't have a beard."

"Well, there isn't much I can do about that yet." He laughed again and rubbed his chin. "But I do run around carrying spears and waving banners, and in *Henry the Fifth* I bring on the cannon."

Jenny was interested. "Tell me more," she said. They passed a cool fountain where massed pink and white blooms perfumed the summer sunshine.

"I was chosen in auditions they hold in the fall," he said. "I'm too young to be a real apprentice, but one day I will be."

Ontario Street was a bustle of tourists. As they walked toward it up a flight of concrete steps, Jenny noticed a garden where trees cast umbrellas of shade over small wooden benches.

"Why don't we sit here for a while?" she suggested.

"I'm in two other plays this season," he said after they sat down. "*The Tempest,* and *King Lear.* But *Henry the Fifth* is my favorite. It's a fine play. It's all about an English king who goes over to conquer France. There's a great battle at a place called Agincourt." He was a restless boy, full of quick gestures. "I play a soldier. We study fencing, you know, so our stage wars look very authentic."

"I wish I knew how to fence!"

"I could teach you. That part was fun. But learning to be an actor is hard work, you know."

"Don't you go to school?"

"Of course. When we start rehearsals in the spring we try to work around our classes, but I still had to make up a lot of lessons."

"Well," Jenny said morosely, "I suppose I'll be going to see you act one of these days. My parents insist that I have to see *everything*. Not all at once, thank goodness. They're going to spread it out over the summer in small doses . . . like an inoculation."

"You don't want to go?"

"No! I don't like Shakespeare. Do you?"

"Now that's a funny question," he said. "I've never even thought of whether or not I like Shakespeare. He's such a big part of my life. Even when I was a baby I never heard lullabies — I heard soliloquies."

"What's that?"

"It's when an actor is supposed to be talking to himself — except the audience can hear his thoughts. That's how my father used to put me to sleep — it was a kind of music." Toby remembered something else. "When we were little kids my sisters and I never used to play cowboys and Indians or stuff like that. We used to act out the murder scene from *Macbeth*, or argue about who would play Hamlet. I always won!" He slashed the air with imaginary swordplay. "Of course I like Shakespeare."

They got up and walked toward the main street. Jenny noticed the morning paper on a newsstand.

"Did you know there was a fire at the theatre last night?" she asked.

"I was there," he said quickly. "It was nothing at all." She could tell by the sudden coldness of his voice that he wanted to change the subject.

"Toby! Toby!" A thin girl in her early teens grabbed him by the back of the shirt. "I've been looking all over for you. Mother's frantic!" Her pale face was peppered with little golden freckles, and her huge eyes were anxious. "You must come right home!"

"What's the matter, Olivia?"

"It's Father. Something awful — please come quickly."

They both dashed off down the street. Toby did not even say goodbye. Jenny wondered if she would ever have a chance to talk to him again.

4

FOR A WHILE Jenny wandered around the business section of the city. She looked into the shining windows of a china shop. Farther along, there were displays of fine linens and the rich woolen goods which were always admired by American tourists. In one gift store there was an interesting group of Eskimo stone carvings — walrus and seal and polar bear. It was even fun for a time to watch the people go in and out of restaurants and to read the menus which were pasted up. But then she began to feel bored and lonesome. She went toward home through the Shakespearean Gardens.

In a way the gardens reminded her of a series of

pleasant and private rooms. The sounds of the city seemed far away. Rectangular plots were set off by stone walls or neat hedges. Small benches had been set in odd little corners to provide a place where one could enjoy the sight and scent of the many-colored blossoms. It was all very peaceful. In the middle of the park was an old stone chimney which soared high in the air, like some staunch sentry determined to preserve the tranquillity below.

As Jenny sat down, her attention was caught by a strange figure moving slowly along the pathways. She was not sure at first whether it was a man or a woman, but as it approached and stooped suddenly to touch a rose she saw that it was a man — an old and rather sad one. His pale face was long and very thin. Untidy gray hair hung uncombed almost to his shoulders. He wore a kind of loose cloak over wretched trousers. Stopping here and there along the path, he made quick sketches in a notebook.

When he came near Jenny he gave her a shy smile. She smiled back.

"There's rosemary." He pointed to a low shrub whose linear leaves were dark green above and white below. "That's for remembrance." He laughed softly and then snapped off a leaf to smell it. "But nobody remembers Evan Montmorency."

Jenny turned the name over in her mind. She said simply, "My mother does."

He looked at her strangely. "I beg your pardon?"

"My mother remembers Evan Montmorency," she repeated. "That's your name, isn't it?"

"Yes," he admitted. "But why should she remember it?"

"Because you are a great actor," Jenny explained. "Both my parents are very fond of the theatre, and I've heard them mention you many times."

Obviously pleased and surprised, the old man sat down beside her.

"As a matter of fact," Jenny went on, "the last time Mother mentioned your name she said 'I wonder whatever became of Evan Montmorency.' Now I'll be able to tell her that you are performing right here in Stratford."

"Oh, no," he said hurriedly. "That wouldn't be true."

"Aren't you with the Festival players?"

"No. I'm only visiting here for the season." His voice poured out like rich molasses. "I'm retired, you see."

"Now that's funny." Jenny chuckled. "You always hear about theatrical people who are *going* to retire, but I never thought any of them actually did it."

"You're a funny little girl," he told her. "Who are you?"

"Jenny McNamara. My father is William McNamara. He's a professor of Speech and Drama, and he's written some books about the theatre. Have you ever heard of him?"

"No, Jenny, I haven't. But I'll tell you a story that might amuse him. It's the true story of an actor who really did retire. Not because he was too old, and certainly not because he was rich enough. It was all because of a hiccup."

"A hiccup?"

"Jenny," he said, "I was an actor long before you were born, perhaps even before your parents were born. A few years ago when I was still in my prime I played the part of King Lear with a big touring company. We went to all the great cities in Canada and the United States, and filled all the grand theatres. Finally we arrived at Toronto — and the Royal Alexandra." His voice dropped dramatically. "It was opening night. Everything went splendidly. The audience literally wrung their hands over the plight of that miserable king, gone mad because of the ingratitude of his daughters. And then I was dying, holding my beloved Cordelia lifeless in my arms . . . knowing at last that she had not betrayed me."

He thrust out long arms, and began to pace quickly up and down the white gravel path.

"*Howl, howl, howl, howl! O, you are men of stones!*
Had I your tongues and eyes, I'd use them so
That heaven's vault should crack. She's gone for ever . . .
Why should a dog, a horse, a rat have life,
And thou no breath at all?"

He dropped to his knees, crouching over an imaginary figure.

"*Thou'lt come no more,*
Never, never, never, never, never."

The actor's voice had dwindled to a whisper. Jenny found herself staring hypnotically at the empty place he was addressing.

"*Pray you undo this button. Thank you, sir.*
Do you see this? Look on her. Look, her lips.
Look there, look there!"

He rose to his feet and returned to the bench.

"Saying that," he said, "I died."

Slowly Jenny released her breath.

"And then I hiccupped."

She waited tensely.

"I hiccupped," the old man repeated. "In that reverent hush, as women wiped their streaming eyes, I hiccupped. It was not a modest hiccup." He shook his head. "It was not timid. I felt very much like Mount Vesuvius must feel after a monumental eruption."

"Then what happened?" Jenny asked.

"I hiccupped again."

High in a tree a bird burst into a song of piercing sweetness. Mr. Montmorency sat down, crossed his thin legs, and drew his cloak tightly around him, although sunlight lay warm across his shoulders. His eyes, deep-set in pockets of gray shadow, gleamed brightly. Jenny saw that he was smiling.

"There was an awful stillness," he continued, "hanging around me like a shroud. Then from the very front row there was a spark of laughter. It began to ripple from seat to seat, and then it ignited and lit that whole confounded audience. The Royal Alexandra was ablaze with laughter. They were laughing at me. At me! It was total and ruinous disgrace."

"And you — "

"I never set foot on the stage again." He tilted back his ravaged face, and the smile in his eyes had vanished. On each side of his mouth were deep ravines, painfully carved.

"How sad," Jenny said. She had a lump in her throat.

But Evan Montmorency brightened up before her eyes.

"Oh, I still have plans," he told her. "When the season is finished in Stratford I hitchhike about. I sketch and paint. I make notes for my memoirs. But every summer I come back to watch these terrible players perform my beloved Shakespeare."

"Do you really think they are terrible?"

His face twisted, as if in pain.

"Terrible? No. They are good — so good that it hurts me." He tapped his bony chest. "Shakespeare's plays don't change. What changes is the way in which they can be performed. Here it is all so bold and creative that I ache to be a part of it. It hurts me because they are so much better than I ever was — could ever be."

"I don't understand," Jenny told him.

"I'm not sure I understand it myself," he said.

"Mr. Montmorency," she asked, "would you please give me your autograph? I think my mother would be proud to have it."

The old man smiled. He stood up and with a grand flourish signed his name on a sheet of his notebook and presented it to her.

5

HOW ABOUT a boat ride this afternoon, honey?"

The professor was pleased with his morning's work. Wearing a flamboyant shirt covered with pink pelicans, he sat down and attacked a lopsided three-decker sandwich.

"That's the second invitation I've had today," Jenny told him. She spooned an extra dollop of mayonnaise over a hill of bacon, lettuce and tomato, and tried to flatten it all out between two slices of bread. Her mother watched wistfully and nibbled a tiny salad. She was usually on a diet.

"Who asked you first?" she asked.

"I met an actor this morning. Except he's really just a boy. And something awful happened to his father right after he asked me to go out in the boat."

"Who is his father?" Dr. McNamara wanted to know.

"Alexander Cardiff." Jenny munched.

"*The* Alexander Cardiff?" Surprised, her mother put down her teacup with a clink. "Oh, dear."

"What happened to him, Jenny?"

"That's the worst part," she said unhappily. "I never did find out. Toby's sister — her name is Olivia — just dashed up, and told him to go straight home. She said it was something *awful*."

"That's odd," her father said. "I talked with Alex for a few minutes this morning over at the theatre. He was perfectly all right then." He looked at his wife. "We met him a few years ago at an opening, remember?"

"Maybe he was hit by a bus," Jenny suggested helpfully. "Or poisoned or something."

"Jenny — " warned her mother. "Don't even think such dreadful things."

"Toby acted funny when I asked him about the fire last night."

"They seemed pretty upset about it at the theatre, too," her father said. "I gather it might not have been accidental. Anyway — they were very nice to me and gave me a lot of useful information for my book."

"But it is rather frightening," said Mrs. Mc-

Namara. "I mean if someone deliberately set the fire. I doubt if it will worry your cousin Cleo, though. She's on her way."

Jenny choked on a piece of bread and had to be pounded on the back.

"That's no way to react," scolded her mother. "Cousin Cleo raised your father, and she did a fine job of it, too." Dr. McNamara radiated modestly. "She also happens to be very fond of you."

"If she loves me so much," Jenny said, "then why does she keep trying to change me?"

"She doesn't want to change you." Her father rumpled her short hair. "*Improve* would be a better word for it. She just wants to make sure that you grow up into a nice, well-behaved young lady."

"Have you told her that I want to be a skydiver?"

Her parents exchanged a brief glance.

"No. And I don't think I'd mention it to her right away," said her mother.

"Will she be staying very long?"

"She said indefinitely on the card," was the reply.

"Oh." Jenny scrubbed her face with a napkin. "We'd better have that boat ride, Daddy. I think I need some fresh air."

"Well, hold your horses. I need nourishment," he told her.

When they arrived at the dock after lunch her father rented a canoe. She had never seen him in one before. At their summer cottage on the Lake of Bays they owned a broad and reassuring rowboat.

"Have you ever paddled one of these before?" She settled herself in the bow and gripped both sides.

"Haven't I ever told you about my jolly Boy Scout days?"

"You never mentioned using a canoe."

He drew confidently on his pipe and examined the paddle in a professional way. "Just relax." He tossed a paper sack between them. "There are some crumbs for you."

"For me? What do I do with them?"

"Feed the swans, of course. Everybody does."

"Good luck." A sunburned man pushed them off and gave them a friendly salute.

"That was a strange thing to say," Jenny said. "Do you suppose he thinks we need it?"

But her father was reminiscing happily. "Yes, this reminds me of my boyhood," he told her. "Staggering up woodland trails with a knapsack on my back. Spending all those hours trying to light bonfires without a match."

"What I'm really interested in," said Jenny, "is whether or not you ever paddled a canoe before today."

The professor was lost in pleasant thoughts. He puffed contentedly and bravely plunged the paddle into the placid waters. The canoe wobbled. Then it began to creep toward the shoreline.

"Small craft warnings are up, Daddy," Jenny said in a very small voice.

Victoria Lake was certainly not very wide. Perhaps

it wasn't deep either — but somehow it seemed vastly threatening. Beautiful homes and tapering lawns were shimmering reflections on the opposite side. Here and there small boys fished hopefully along the bank, under giant willows which trailed their heavy hair in the water.

Once more Dr. McNamara firmly applied his paddle. This time they changed course. Jenny could see that her father was getting down to business. She relaxed a little.

"What is that building, Daddy?"

"Exhibition Hall. That's the Arena next to it."

"What do they exhibit?"

"Oh, different things each year. Rare and contemporary books, for instance . . . usually some Canadiana — arts, crafts and so forth. They always have a display of costumes and props from last season's performances. You'll enjoy it."

Jenny stared at all the people who crowded the picnic tables at the edge of the water. The canoe wavered toward a little island situated just where the lake began to narrow into the Avon River.

"The swans! There they are!" A group of great white birds floated on the surface nearby. Sunlight glistened on their impeccable vests. As they dipped supple necks to snatch at crumbs, it was a ballet of grace and greed. Their young, the cygnets, were downy balls of buff, just as ravenous as their parents.

"May I feed them now?" Jenny leaned over the side of the canoe.

"Wait a minute. I'll try to get a little closer."

One determined paddle thrust sent them right into the middle of the banquet. It was like landing in a snowbank.

"Now," said Dr. McNamara.

Jenny made a grab for the paper bag. Her long legs knocked against the side of the boat.

"Jenny, be careful!"

It was too late. The red canoe wobbled violently and tipped over. Jenny's shriek was rudely cut off as a pane of cold water broke over her head. When she came up gasping, a swan dived boldly at her nose. Breadcrumbs bobbed all around. Thrashing wildly, water and weeds streaming down her face, she managed to stand up, and was embarrassed to find that the water just reached above her knees.

"It's not deep," said a woman's strong voice. "Don't be frightened. Just take my hand."

"It's cold," Jenny stammered.

"Then take my hand and climb out."

Her rescuer, a stout lady with a dab of mustard on her chin, extended a helpful arm. Jenny grabbed hold of it and hauled herself out of the river.

Looking back, she could see her father sitting in water up to his neck. His pipe, still in place, was no longer smoking. His hat was on. The canoe, half submerged, rested quietly nearby, but the paddle had floated away. With massive dignity, as if just emerging from his morning bath, the professor drew himself up out of the Avon.

There was excited conversation among the many spectators. At the nearest picnic table, a girl with long, pale red hair burst into wild giggles. She clapped both hands over her mouth to cram back the sound, but laughter still shook out like loose coins spilling. Her face turned bright pink, but she could not stop laughing.

"That's enough, Sarah." The stout lady spoke sharply. She gestured toward a sandwich which a small, baldheaded man was still holding in midair. "Put it down, Sam, and help me get these unfortunate people home."

Briskly she removed all the paper dishes from the top of the table and then whipped off the checkered cloth. This she wrapped around Jenny. The redhaired girl subsided into little whistling gasps. She sounded like a coffeepot that had just been whisked off the stove.

"Drive them home, Sam."

Jenny had certainly not enjoyed her afternoon swim. Her teeth rattled like a typewriter. She paused long enough to bestow a devastating glare on Sarah, and then she followed the lady with the mustard on her chin.

6

IT WAS TERRIBLE. It was just terrible."

Jenny sat in the kitchen with a towel wrapped around her head. She nibbled at a pickle. Dill pickles, the fat ones with warts, always soothed her best.

"It was utterly humiliating."

Mrs. McNamara found it hard to reply. Her mouth was all puckered up from watching her daughter. "Well, it was very nice of the Americans to bring you home," she managed. "From New York City. That's what the little redheaded girl told me."

"That girl," Jenny fumed. "It was bad enough having hundreds of people staring at me. But she laughed out loud."

"Well— it must have been quite a spectacle. I wish I'd been there." Her mother's brown eyes were full of laughter.

"And those horrible swans. All they did was eat, eat, eat. One of them almost got my nose."

"What did you expect the poor things to do?" Mrs. McNamara asked.

"Daddy said he'd been a Boy Scout," Jenny grumbled, "but I'll bet he never got a merit badge for boating."

"No, I won an award for Indian dancing. I remember it well." The professor joined them. He also had a towel draped over his head, trailing down over his shoulders so that he looked like a rakish sheik in gay Bermuda shorts. He began to hop around the kitchen in an impromptu Eagle dance. "It was you," he reminded Jenny, "who tipped the boat."

"I know." She grinned around the pickle, snapped off a bite, and crunched heartily. "It was all my fault."

"Please stop panting and sit down, Bill," said Mrs. McNamara. "You're making me nervous. Why don't you see what you can do with the refrigerator."

"I thought Humphrey was supposed to fix it."

"He's been holed up in his workshop all morning," she sighed. "His mother assured me he can fix anything. She says he's an inventor."

The Dumphries lived in the downstairs apartment.

"Then our refrigerator shouldn't be such a challenge to his genius."

They heard a gentle tap at the door.

"Maybe that's him now," said Mrs. McNamara. But it was not the raisin-puddingface. A very small, very bleached, very timid young man peeped in at them over the metal rims of his glasses. He was the oldest-looking young man she had ever laid eyes on. His hair, which was brushed forward until it touched his eyebrows, was so light that it looked almost white. His little body was tightly buttoned into an old man's conservative suit. She was surprised to see that he was not wearing shoes and that his socks were soggy.

"I seem to be having a bit of trouble. May I use your telephone?"

"Of course," Mrs. McNamara said. "Please come in."

Printing little patterns on the floor, the visitor advanced damply into the room. "I don't have a telephone myself," he told them. "When you have one, then people keep calling you up."

Dr. McNamara made introductions.

"I'm Dylan Forde. I live in the next apartment, and my kitchen is flooded."

"Oh, dear!"

"Have you spoken to Mr. Dumphrie about it?" asked Jenny's father.

"There doesn't seem to be anyone at home right now."

"Then I'd better call you a plumber right away." Mrs. McNamara reached for the phone book.

"That would be most kind. It's rather sloppy in there."

"Sit down," urged the professor. "Maggie will straighten things out for you in no time. You're the actor, aren't you?"

"Yes. Yes, I am." Mr. Forde fixed his eyes steadfastly on one corner of the kitchen ceiling.

"We've enjoyed all your performances so much." Mrs. McNamara riffled through the yellow pages.

"Thank you." His worried face rearranged itself into a diminutive smile.

"How did your kitchen get flooded?" Jenny asked.

"It's very strange, "Mr. Forde said, addressing the wastebasket. "I slept quite late, and was awakened when a friend of mine came calling."

"We met her!" Jenny was enthusiastic. "It was Sybilla!"

He allowed his little smile to expand into a very large one. "You met Sybilla? Isn't she spectacular?"

"She certainly is."

"It was after she left that the kitchen sink began to overflow," he told them. "It just kind of threw up."

"Tell me," said Dr. McNamara, "Was there an accident at the theatre today? We heard that Alexander Cardiff was involved in something."

Dylan Forde expressed genuine surprise.

"I haven't heard a thing about it," he said. "But then I haven't been out of the house yet."

"We hope it isn't anything serious." Maggie Mc-

Namara underlined a number in the phone book. "The show must go on, mustn't it?"

"I wish it would go on without me!" was the furious reply. The actor glared at the electric clock. There was an astonished silence. Dylan Forde looked surprised at himself.

"I don't mean that exactly," he admitted. "It's just that I'm so sick and tired of being an old man."

"An old man? Why, you're young," Jenny said.

"Then why must I always, always play old men?" He began to pace rapidly up and down the room. "I've been Polonius I don't know how many times. Even in high school I played Polonius. Every single part that requires a white wig or a quaver is mine. I'm only surprised that I've never yet been cast as Juliet's nurse."

"But you do those parts so well — " said Mrs. McNamara.

"Don't you think I could be Antony? Don't you suppose I am a Hamlet?"

He hopped up on a kitchen chair, and held his chest as if he clutched an inner pain. Then Dylan Forde's voice clamored like a carrillon.

> *"I am dead, Horatio. Wretched queen, adieu!*
> *You that look pale and tremble at this chance,*
> *That are but mutes or audience to this act,*
> *Had I but time, as this fell sergeant Death*
> *Is strict in his arrest, O, I could tell you —*
> *But let it be. Horatio, I am dead:*

Thou livest; report me and my cause aright
To the unsatisfied."

His breath slowly oozed out like smoke from under a tight door. Dylan Forde toppled off the chair and crashed to the floor. Jenny gasped. Her mother dropped the telephone receiver.

"There." Satisfied with himself, the actor sat up pertly. "I think I play Hamlet very well."

They applauded loudly. He sat down again in one neat little movement, his legs dangling over the edge of the chair.

"The hardest part to bear," he confided to the stove, "is that Sybilla thinks I'm too *young*. She cooks me things that are *good* for me . . . things I don't like. She makes my dental appointments, and mothers me. Smothers me, in fact. But she won't marry me. It's very discouraging."

Mrs. McNamara hung up the telephone. "The plumber will be right over," she announced cheerfully.

"The last time I saw Sybilla was in Toronto," the actor told them. "After that the garbage disposal wouldn't work for three days." Already he looked brighter. He thanked them politely and padded off toward the door, where he suddenly stopped.

"Remarkable woman, isn't she?" he said.

"Magnificent!" Jenny's laughter bubbled over. "She told us so herself."

Dylan Forde allotted himself one tiny chuckle, and departed.

"What a peculiar young man." Amused, Maggie McNamara shook her head over him. Jenny put an arm around her mother's waist.

"I'll say one thing for Stratford," she said. "It's certainly not dull!"

7

TOBY! Hey — Toby!"

Jenny had borrowed a bicycle from Humphrey. It was in bad shape. It clanked and rattled with every turn of the wheels. Toby was strolling along the footpath at the edge of the Avon River when she caught sight of him.

"Where did you get that thing?"

"Well, it *is* noisy . . ." she dragged her feet to stop the bike, "but it gets me places." She smiled at him. "I've been looking for you. How is your father?"

Toby looked at her strangely. "He's fine."

"But the other day when your sister came rushing up to get you she said . . ."

"Oh, *that.*" He stared out over the calm water. "Olivia's very emotional."

"But she was frightened."

"My father hasn't missed a performance in years. Don't worry about him. I said he was fine."

Jenny closed her mouth. She felt hurt. "Well, I have to be going." She climbed back on the bicycle.

"Wait a minute." His tone thawed a little. "Why don't you park that thing somewhere and come for a walk? I'm going over to the island."

She hesitated only a second. "All right."

It was still early in the morning. The day was fresh and unclouded; it smelled new and clean. Theatre-goers and picnickers had not started to arrive. The little island Toby mentioned was connected to the mainland by a red, humpbacked bridge. As they crossed over Jenny admired the neatly trimmed shrubs and bushes. Palette-shaped flower beds held bunches of color where blossoms glowed like vivid strokes of paint. They sat down on one of the benches facing the Festival Theatre.

"Have you seen a play yet?" Toby asked.

"No. But tonight we see good old *Henry the Fifth.*"

"Don't forget to watch for me."

"O.K. How come you get up so early in the morning? I thought actors always slept late after working at night. Mr. Forde does."

"I like to get up early. It gives me a chance to be alone — to think about things. Sometimes I have to be over at the theatre. Did you say Forde?"

"Dylan Forde. He lives in the next apartment."

"Poor Dylan. What's been happening to him lately?"

"His kitchen flooded."

Toby laughed out loud. He looked friendly and pleasant again.

"Sybilla must be in town."

"How did you know that?"

"Because things happen when Sybilla is around. Bathtubs overflow. Dogs howl. Mailmen go on strike."

"Calamity!" Jenny giggled.

"That's it. Calamity." This time they both laughed together. It felt good to warm themselves in the sunshine. Companionably they watched a fleet of swans sailing toward a man who had just emerged from behind one of the trees. His hands were stretched out hospitably toward the birds as he tossed bread into the water.

"I know him." Jenny stood up abruptly. She waved her arms. "Mr. Montmorency! Hello."

The old man stared in their direction. He was a fantastic sight. His face was grotesquely daubed with greasepaint, his hair wildly awry, some of it caught in a crumpled Elizabethan ruff which was fastened around his neck. He wore an ancient jacket of orange and black over worn tights which had been mended all over. His boots were practically falling apart. Jenny was dismayed at the sight of him.

But Evan Montmorency was perfectly delighted with himself. He was charmed to see them. Bidding a gracious goodbye to the swans as he flung them one last handful of breakfast, he bowed deeply in Jenny's direction and sang,

> "*A great while ago the world begun*
> *With hey, ho, the wind and the rain,*
> *But that's all one, our play is done,*
> *And we'll strive to please you every day.*"

Then he came toward them.

"Good morning," said Jenny.

"It's a delicious morning. And how are you, dear Sir Toby?"

The boy's face flushed, and then closed itself into an angry mask.

"I have to go, Jenny," he told her. "I'll see you around."

"Sit down and chat awhile with an old man," invited the actor cordially.

But Toby turned and headed back toward the bridge.

"Wait a minute." Mr. Montmorency spoke out in such ringing and imperious tones that Jenny felt he could stop church bells from chiming if he put his mind to it.

Toby turned. He planted his hands stubbornly in his pockets.

"No time for old friends?" the actor challenged him.

Toby looked as if he had just swallowed something bitter.

"No time for old fools!" His voice choked. He turned and retreated, his back a rigid insult.

"Toby!" Jenny was shocked. "What's the matter with you?"

"Never mind. Never mind. Never, never mind," repeated Mr. Montmorency softly. All the morning mirth and song had gone out of him. "Sticks and stones, you know," he murmured with a kind of weary humor. "Let him go. Let him go."

"But he was rude." She watched the frail and papery fingers lace and interlace among themselves. "I didn't know that you knew Toby."

"I've known him since he was a matter of a few minutes old," he explained. "I gave him his name."

"You did?"

"Yes," the old man said proudly. "The Cardiffs weren't expecting a boy. After all, they already had Rosalind, Viola, Olivia and Portia. So when a son came along they were completely unprepared. I took one look at the fat little fellow in his nightgown, and told his mother that there was a Sir Toby Belch if I'd ever seen one. She quite agreed."

"Sir Toby Belch?"

"One of Shakespeare's drunken knaves, my dear. But lovable."

"And he's still angry with you for that?"

His eyes, under a frosted tangle of eyebrows, were genuinely pained and puzzled.

"No, not for that. Toby and I have been devoted friends for years. But lately I've discovered that the boy is annoyed or ashamed — maybe both. Of course his parents are always kind, but I seldom go to see them . . . not since I've retired."

"Well, I'm ashamed of him." Jenny was still indignant. "Goodbye, Mr. Montmorency. There's something I have to do."

Once she looked back at the lonely figure on the bench, but he had already forgotten her. He stared wistfully after the swans drifting away down the river. By the time she picked up her bike and pumped it noisily up the hill toward the theatre, Toby was already a distant figure cutting across the lawn.

"Toby!' she cried. "You wait for me."

He kept right on walking.

"Toby!" This time she yelled. Reluctantly he turned and waited as she churned to a stop. She wheeled the bike toward him, thinking he looked ashamed of himself.

"Well — Sir Toby Belch!" she exploded. "How dare you be so rude to a friend of mine — and of yours?"

"What right have you to stick your nose into other people's business anyway?" he replied angrily. "You don't know anything."

"What don't I know?"

"That Evan Montmorency is not only probably crazy — but he may be dangerous as well."

"That poor old man," she scoffed.

"You'd better watch your step, Jenny. You might wind up like everyone in our family."

"And how is that?"

"Scared." He said the word slowly and distinctly. "Scared to death."

Jenny's heart began a slow wallop inside her. Toby leaned forward until they stared solemnly into each other's wide open eyes.

"But why?" she said.

"Maybe you'll get a letter in your mailbox — a letter that says this will be your last summer in Stratford," he said. "Or maybe your telephone will ring, and when you answer it there won't be anyone there . . . just the sound of breathing. Or someone will heave a brick through your window in the middle of the night. Things like that are frightening, Jenny. And you won't even be sure whom you are frightened of."

"And you think — " she swallowed — "that sad man down there . . ."

"I have *reason* to think . . ." he began.

"Toby!" It was his sister Olivia, whom Jenny had seen before. She smiled, and tugged her brother's ear. "Mother said if I saw you to remind you about the salami and rye bread. Bring your friend, if you like. She can stay for lunch."

Toby opened his mouth to protest, but Jenny was too quick for him. Curiosity stinging, she said, "Why thank you. I'd love to come."

8

THE HOUSE on Queen Street was very large and very old. It belonged to a pair of spinster schoolteachers. These elderly ladies had an affectionate interest in the Cardiffs. Each year when they departed for a long vacation in their little sports car, they rented their house with all its antiques and curios to the distinguished actor and his family.

"Is everyone dressed? Company coming!" Olivia shouted into the dark front hall. There was no reply. She gestured for Jenny to follow her. Inside was a cage of pleasant confusion. In the living room several bold parakeets fussed and twittered. There was loud audience laughter and applause behind the cold eye of a television set which no one watched. Continuous static crackled from a neglected radio.

It was also a house of clocks; a ticking, gonging house. As they came in they heard the crazy call of cuckoos. Little wooden birds popped from every wall piping out the hour. One clock contained a miniature old woman who stuck her worried face out of a door with strenuous regularity. There was a massive grandfather clock which stood like an upended coffin in the hall. Over all the sounds of time came laughter and the clink of dishes being washed.

"Mother?" Olivia pushed into the kitchen, with Jenny and Toby at her heels. The kitchen was old-fashioned, and flooded with sunlight. Toby's teenage sisters chattered by the sink. Both Rosalind and Viola wore their thick, copper-bright hair brushed into long bangs. A chameleon dozed on Rosalind's shoulder, and on top of the breadbox was a wire container where a brisk little hamster warmed up on his exercise wheel. Two cats churned forward and wove themselves into purring collars around Jenny's ankles.

Mrs. Cardiff was a very beautiful lady who smelled of carnations. Her dark violet eyes never seemed to be quite in focus.

"Mother — this is Jenny McNamara. She's a friend of Toby's, and we've invited her for lunch."

Toby remarked pointedly, "Olivia invited her."

Mrs. Cardiff smiled at Jenny. "Well, I'm glad she did." She was mixing something sticky in a bowl. Her delicate long hands wandered constantly toward her hair and left it stuck here and there with silvery patches.

"Her father's a professor," Olivia announced. "He's writing a book about the theatre, and he's going to put us all in it."

Jenny had not said this exactly.

"Oh, really?" Once more Mrs. Cardiff dabbed at her hair. "Now that's very exciting."

Rosalind spoke up. Like Olivia she was peppered with little freckles. Two dimples were buried deeply on each side of her mouth. "But that's marvelous. All about us — imagine!" She lowered her voice. "Tell me, Jenny . . . aren't professors rather peculiar people?"

"Rosie," warned her mother, "please don't be rude."

"But that's not rude," Rosalind insisted. "That's just being curious. I happen to know a lot about professors. They're very intelligent, aren't they, Jenny?"

"I suppose so," Jenny thought it over. "Although with Daddy it really doesn't show."

"Here's the salami, Mom." Toby tossed a package on the table, and looked hopefully into the mixing bowl. "What's that?"

"Just paste. The girls and I are going to finish making our papier-mâché puppets this afternoon."

"We're going to put on a show for the neighborhood kids," Viola explained. "Maybe you'd like to help us." She was a couple of years older than her brother, with big dreamy eyes. She continually blew up her bangs so she could see.

Under their feet an unholy racket suddenly broke out. Jenny thought the whole house was under attack. Then there came a rhythmical bang, bang, bang, and she realized that someone was practicing on a set of drums.

"It's only Portia," said Rosalind, raising her voice. "She's very musical. We make her practice in the cellar."

"She's very noisy," Toby complained. "I wish we'd left either her or the drums at home."

"It does get kind of crowded," Viola said vaguely, wiping plates. "I mean that station wagon just isn't big enough for all of us. We ought to hire a moving van."

"Viola exaggerates," Mrs. Cardiff said, "but it is getting to be more of a problem each year. And Rosie insisted on bringing Hamlet."

Toby held his nose. "That hamster smells," he said.

"Hamlet is fastidious!" Rosalind was indignant. "Even Father says so. Ask him."

"Where is he, anyway?"

Mrs. Cardiff shook her head. "Don't bother him, Toby. He's upstairs reading the stock market report, and you know how that upsets him."

Someone was calling at the back entrance.

"Yoo-hoooooooo! Anybody here?" It was a husky and memorable voice. Jenny recognized it at once.

"Sybilla." Olivia dashed to open the screen door.

It was definitely Sybilla. She was mysteriously dressed in black jacket and pants, with a large helmet pulled over her ears. Her face was almost hidden by a sinister pair of dark goggles.

Toby burst into a sudden passion of laughter. "You look like Ant Lady in the comics!"

She ignored him. "Guess what I've bought?"

"Oh, dear," Mrs. Cardiff murmured, "not another camel, Sybilla?"

"Of course not, darling. It's a motorcycle," she crowed.

"A motorcycle!" Toby hurtled out the door. He popped back in long enough to give Sybilla a fierce hug. "You don't look like Ant Lady at all. You look like her gorgeous younger sister."

"Oh, Sybilla," Mrs. Cardiff reproached her, "he'll want to ride it. He'll break his neck."

Their visitor exuded stupendous confidence. "Don't worry, there's nothing to it. I'll teach him myself." She removed her goggles, and lifted off the helmet. "After all," she said, "I've had it for hours and nothing has happened to *me*." She recognized Jenny. "Hello, there. How are you, sweetie?"

Jenny said she was just fine.

"Have you met Dylan yet?"

"Yes. His sink overflowed, and he wanted to use our telephone."

Wild laughter. "Poor Dylan. He's really such a baby. He can't take care of himself, you know."

"You never give him the chance," Mrs. Cardiff protested gently.

"I haven't seen Alex yet. Does he know I'm in town?" Sybilla asked.

"Martha!" There was an outraged bellow from the top of the stairs, a furious clatter of footsteps, and Alexander Cardiff exploded into the kitchen.

"He does now," said his wife.

Jenny saw a tall and splendid man, wonderfully handsome and dressed as chastely as a clergyman. His beard was so severely groomed that it looked as if he starched it.

"My stock has dropped ten points." He shoved a crumpled newspaper under his wife's elegant nose.

"You know I can't see without my glasses," she told him. "And you haven't met Jenny McNamara yet, or even said hello to Sybilla."

Jenny shook hands, and Sybilla tilted up her cheek to catch his kiss.

"I should have guessed you were in Stratford," he said wryly.

"Alex, dearest," she pouted. "I thought everyone knew I was in town."

He threw up his hands in surrender. "Yesterday my stock was up ten points."

"I never read the newspapers," she told him airily, "and so up or down it's all the same to me."

"But not to me." Looking pained, he cautiously sat down. "Are you going to be here long?"

"Weeks and weeks and weeks, I hope." She stretched luxuriously. "I have a singing engagement at the Fare Thee Well."

"That's a local coffeehouse," Viola explained to Jenny.

Alexander Cardiff appealed to his wife. "I'll be ruined!"

The front doorbell and the telephone rang simultaneously. Rosalind headed for the front door, while her father went into an alcove in the hall. Sybilla dipped her little finger into the mixing bowl and licked it daintily. She made a face. "Good heavens, darling," she said, "but that's terrible."

"It's only paste, Sybilla," Mrs. Cardiff said. "It doesn't have to taste good." They were all laughing when Rosalind bounced back with a florist's box.

"It's for you, Mother."

"But it can't be for me." Martha Cardiff was as excited as a girl. "It's not my birthday — not an anniversary."

In the hall her husband demanded: "Who is this?"

There was a deep silence. Portia had stopped banging the drums.

The bouquet of flowers inside the box was a disgusting sight. The roses had been left to molder and decay in a damp place. No one spoke. Even Sybilla, for once, found nothing to say.

Mr. Cardiff came back into the kitchen. He walked heavily as if he hurt.

"Someone wanted to know if you liked the flowers, Martha." He looked into the box, and then put an arm around his wife. "It was *him*."

She turned her face to his. "Alex, I can't take much more of this."

"It's going to stop. It has to stop." His voice was positive and stern. Downstairs, Portia slowly began to beat the drums again. Jenny saw Toby's anxious face flash at the screen door.

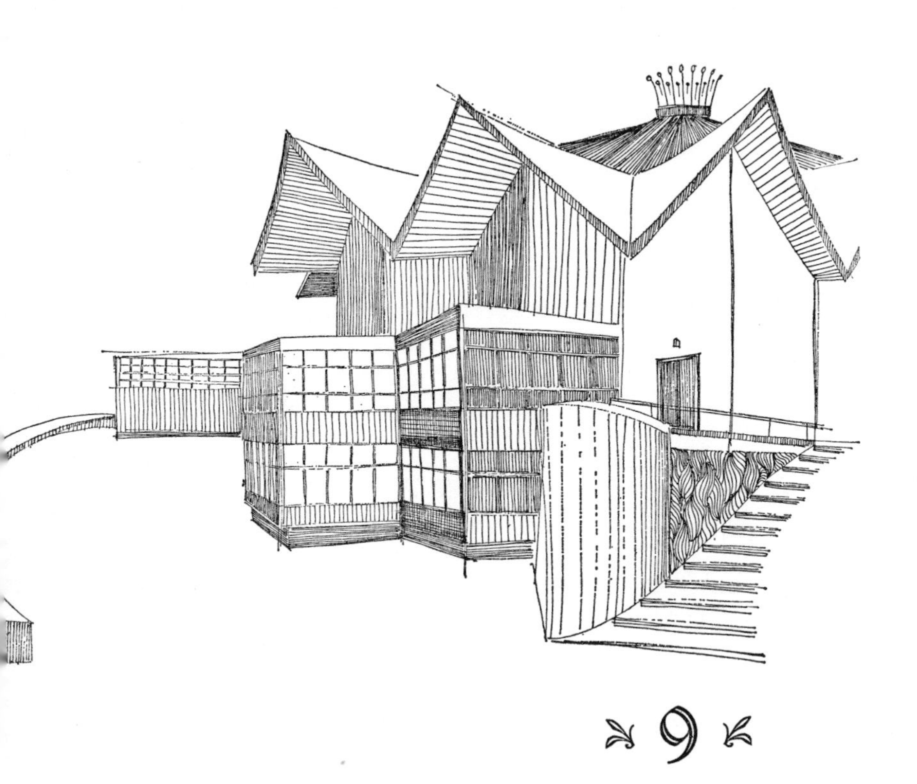

9

AS SHE DRESSED that night for the evening performance of *Henry the Fifth*, Jenny thought about Toby. She had not stayed for lunch with his family after all. Sensing that the delivery of the dead flowers had upset them all greatly, she had made her apologies and scurried home. It was, she realized, only another event in a series of harassments. Something strange was happening in Stratford this summer.

Tonight she would go to the Festival Theatre for the first time. "How will I understand what is happening in the play?" she asked her mother.

Mrs. McNamara, fastening her pearls in front of

the bedroom mirror, smiled at Jenny's frowning reflection.

"Well, you can read the program notes. That will give you a good idea of the plot and the characters. Henry the Fifth was a much-admired English king who felt it was necessary to go and conquer France."

"Why did he think it was necessary?"

Her mother laughed. "I've forgotten why," she said.

"He probably thought it would make a good play sometime." Jenny flopped down on the bed. "How am I going to understand all that fancy language?"

"Well, it's English, for goodness' sakes," Maggie McNamara explained. "Graceful English . . . beautiful English, that's true. Some words will be strange to you, of course. But what your ear can't understand, your eye will interpret."

Jenny scowled. "I'm not so sure," she grumbled. "Besides, I've never thought of history as being very exciting."

"People are exciting," her mother said. "And history *is* people, after all."

"People can also be boring," Jenny complained. "I have the feeling I'm going to be bored silly tonight."

"If you are," her mother replied crisply, "it will be your own fault, not Shakespeare's!"

It was the warm, worn end of the day, and they had decided at dinner to walk to the theatre. As they strolled along the footpath by Victoria Lake, Jenny spotted a white drift of swans floating serenely on the water. She and the birds exchanged a hostile glance; then they turned their proud necks and sailed toward friendlier territory. Jenny talked about her meeting with the Cardiff family, and how it had ended.

"Toby admitted that something spooky is going on. His family have been getting weird phone calls and mean letters. Then today his mother got those horrible dead flowers. Maybe the person who is bothering them is the same one who tried to set that fire at the theatre."

Mrs. McNamara was alarmed. "Do you think so, Bill?" She appealed to her husband. "Do you think there's any real danger?"

"Now stop worrying," he told her. "If that fire was deliberate, then it was meant to frighten people — not to hurt anybody. The theatre is, after all, practically indestructible."

Jenny was unusually observant as they approached the Festival Theatre from below the hill. Her mother had said that people were exciting, and the crowd that flowed toward the evening's entertainment certainly proved her point. Some of the women were extravagantly beautiful in their lovely gowns. There were foreign gentlemen in native costumes; gay, giggling girls in brief skirts; Englishmen with frosty accents and brisk wives; casual old ladies in fat flowered dresses; studious men with thick glasses and severe noses; whooping theatrical youngsters who greeted their friends as if they had been parted for years. The conversation was a percolating discussion of weather and of dinner, news events, gossip and critical analysis. Jenny's ears, sharpened by the events of the past few days, still caught an undertow of rumor — the whispered suspicion of arson.

Pulled into this stream, the McNamaras let themselves be jostled through a bustling lobby, and from there into a curving inner aisle. Jenny was so enchanted by the handsome young usher that when he showed them to their seats she sat down in the bony lap of a dignified lady. The woman uttered a great birdlike squawk, and Jenny flew off with a gasp of apology.

"Well?" They were finally settled, and her mother nudged her expectantly. "What do you think of it?"

Jenny looked around. The magnificent stage was a broad wooden structure which jutted out into a semicircle of over two thousand seats. At the rear five sturdy pillars supported a platform which formed a portico, and a flight of stairs on each side gave easy access to it. There were entrances angled on either side of the stage and at the back of the portico on both levels.

"I think I've seen something like it before," she said.

"You've seen some of my books on the Elizabethan stage," Dr. McNamara said, turning to a page in the glossy souvenir program. "Look, this is a picture of the Globe. Most of Shakespeare's plays were presented there."

"It's — let me see — an octagon on the outside,"

Jenny said. "An octagon has eight sides, doesn't it?"

"Yes. And it's circular on the inside. If you listen carefully to the opening lines of the play you'll hear the actor describe the Globe as 'this wooden O.' "

"See how the old Elizabethan stage projects into the audience," said her mother. "The Festival Theatre is really a very modern adaptation."

"The Globe held almost as many people as this one does," the professor pointed out. "But it was a daylight theatre. There was no electricity then, and so the plays were performed there in the afternoon."

Jenny looked intently at the picture. "Why are all those people standing down in front?"

"Those are the groundlings, or the poorer classes. They paid a penny to stand in the pit."

"And up there — in the balconies?"

"Those are threepenny patrons. They sat on stools. For a shilling you could sit right on the stage."

Jenny looked around her at the wide, whispering tiers of tiny faces. "Can everybody here see what is going on?"

"Yes," replied her mother. "You watch and see how the action of the play keeps flowing all the time — from right to left and left to right, front to back, up and down the stairs. It's almost like a dance. That way everyone has an opportunity to see and hear all the players."

"Hello there. All dried out, I hope?" It was the deep cheerful voice of the woman who had helped Jenny out of the Avon River. She sat almost directly in front of them, between her little husband and red-haired daughter.

"Yes, thank you," Jenny said. The girl turned around and smiled. Her face was homely and friendly. She gestured towards the broad and beautiful lines of the stage.

"Do you get as excited as me?"

"This is my first time," Jenny said, not smiling back, "and I'm not excited at all."

"They don't use scenery, you know — just costumes and props to get the effect, the way they did in Shakespeare's day."

"I know," said Jenny, who didn't.

"There are nine entrances," Sarah Kaplan went on. "And even a trap door right out in the middle of the stage. You can hardly see the actors coming and going. There are ramps which lead to tunnels underneath — they can get artillery on and off quickly that way."

Jenny yawned.

"Won't you join us later at our apartment?" Maggie McNamara leaned forward to speak softly to Mrs. Kaplan. "We'd like to thank you properly for your kindness the other day."

"We'd be delighted," the stout lady replied. "Wouldn't we, Sam?" She sharply elbowed her husband, who blinked his eyes very fast and nodded his head.

"Shhhhhhh," Mrs. Kaplan reprimanded them. "It's beginning."

The audience stood for the national anthem. Then Alexander Cardiff slipped out to the roof of the portico, sat down near the edge, and crossed his handsome legs. Looking out, he quietly spoke the opening lines of the play as a "chorus to history," just as some anonymous actor had first spoken them over three hundred and fifty years ago. He implored the audience to ignore the limitations of the theatre and the players, to use their imagination to encompass the magnitude of the battles to be fought. Then he urged them "gently to hear, kindly to judge" the play.

In spite of herself Jenny could feel her imagination catching fire. First her attention was caught by the sculptured richness of the Archbishop's cloak and then dazzled by a dance of steel on steel during seconds of swordplay. Soldiers leaped and bounded up and down scaling ladders. She thought she recognized Toby at one point. It was not difficult to follow the career of the young English king to his triumph on the field of Agincourt. Jenny was fascinated by the charming French princess Katherine, to whom Henry had pledged his love. The actress was a slight woman, her dark hair almost concealed under a nun-like headdress, but when she spoke her voice soared out with ringing clarity.

"Well?" At the end her mother nudged her again. "How did you like it?"

"I don't know." Mechanically Jenny clapped her hands together, adding another beat to the swelling applause. She felt saturated in violence and beauty.

She needed time to think about the splendor she had witnessed.

A slap of late evening air freshened their faces as they stopped under the balcony just outside.

"Why don't we wait for the Kaplans here," suggested Mrs. McNamara. They had lost sight of their friends in the crowd.

10

JENNY did not sleep well. Dreams, in brash color, thundered in her head all night. Knights jousted with gigantic swans in flower beds which turned into fire. Twice she awakened and found herself groping under the bed for breadcrumbs. In the morning she felt miserable.

Her mother was carrying on her daily battle with the toaster. The bread kept jiggling up and down.

"Mrs. Kaplan just called," she said. "Daddy wants to take you over to the theatre with him this morning, and after lunch I'd like you to go and see Sarah."

"Do I have to go? She laughed at me!"

"Sarah isn't feeling very well today and I told Mrs. Kaplan you would stop by."

"Every minute of my life is planned for me," Jenny complained. "I might as well be a Communist."

After breakfast she clattered downstairs to wait for her father on the porch. Their landlady, Mrs. Dumphrie, was already out sweeping off the steps. She was a dumpy woman of uncertain shape, with gray hair pulled up like a hard ball of string on top of her head. It made Jenny wince just to look at it.

"Good morning."

"Morning." Mrs. Dumphrie stopped sweeping, and peered up at the sky. "Nice day."

"It's going to rain this afternoon," said Humphrey. His great bulk was wedged into a small rocking chair. He always listened to the weather reports.

His mother pursed her lips. "Wasn't smart enough to graduate from high school," she said, "and he can't hold down a decent job . . . but he thinks he knows it all."

Humphrey ignored her. "Where are you going?" he asked Jenny. He always wanted to know where she was going.

"Daddy is taking me over to the Festival Theatre."

"Oh." Mrs. Dumphrie looked as if she suddenly had indigestion. "Over *there*."

"We're going backstage."

"Well . . ." the landlady was philosophical. "I guess some folks like that sort of thing."

"I don't really want to go," Jenny confided.

"Daddy thinks I should. He says it will be educational."

"Uh huh." Mrs. Dumphrie leaned on her broom and stared strangely off into the distance. She seemed to see something rare and revolting. "They're not like us, are they, son?"

He cleared his throat with a noisy rattle. "Nope."

"Stratford's not like it used to be, either. Is it, Humphrey?"

The fat fellow gravely considered the question, and then delivered his sullen opinion. "Nope."

His mother sighed. "It used to be so peaceful here . . . not too many strangers . . . everybody knew everybody else. Now that's all been changed. The Festival did it."

Humphrey grunted. A fly had settled on his nose, and rocked comfortably back and forth with him.

"Of course late in the fall things get back to normal." Mrs. Dumphrie looked more cheerful. "All those odd people go away, and then we have peace and quiet for a while. Still, it's not like the old days. It won't ever be the same again."

Jenny felt uncomfortable. She was surprised to discover that the presence of the Festival might be resented. As she walked along with her father she asked him about it.

"Why do the Dumphries feel that way?"

"Because there are always some people who resent change," he told her. "They don't understand it — they're probably a little afraid of it. Shakespeare has made quite an impact on their lives, besides giving them an opportunity to rent rooms, for which they don't appear to be very grateful. The Dumphries just happen to be rather small-minded people who aren't able to comprehend or tolerate the many worlds beyond their own little one."

"I know a word for that," she said. "*Bigot.*"

"It's a good word," he agreed, "for a sad situation. And here we are."

The administrative offices of the Festival Theatre simmered with activity. Telephones jangled continuously. Miss Charlene Timchuk, an assistant to the director of public relations, greeted them with generous enthusiasm. She was a big girl with a tangled mop of hair and warm brown eyes. She pumped their hands and said that she had been expecting them.

"Miss Timchuk . . ." A nervous-looking man under a blue beret rushed up and pushed a thick envelope into her arms. "Evidence, Miss Timchuk. Fresh evidence."

"I can't see you just now, Mr. Smallwood," she said pleasantly.

He drew closer. "This proves," he hissed, hurling out each word like a hot pebble, "that William Shakespeare did not write *Othello* or *Antony and Cleopatra* or *Richard the Third*. William Shakespeare was, in fact, a fraud."

She handed him back the envelope with a smile. "We'll talk about it later," she promised. "This way please, Dr. McNamara."

They followed her into a series of corridors. Jenny could hear muffled shouts.

"That's an understudy rehearsal onstage," Miss Timchuk explained. "Since each role has an understudy, there are continuous rehearsals going on all season."

They glanced up at the black and silver shields laid out like playing cards on both walls, with a spear fastened next to each one.

"As big as the theatre is," she told them, "storage is always a problem. This way the actors can pick up their shields as they go onstage and replace them on the way back." She opened a door. "Here's our large wardrobe room . . . at least it looks large when it's empty. You ought to see it when thirty people are working . . . one expert creating hats over there . . . another making jewelry at that table . . . seamstresses sewing up costumes over there." She pointed to the clutter of sewing machines and idle dressmaker forms; the boxes of beads; the rainbow of spools. "It's a mess, all right. But wait until you see what comes out of here."

She led them down the hall past a small office. Inside, a bent man studied a sheaf of sketches.

"That's one of our designers," she whispered. "He makes a sketch based on his knowledge of what would be correct for the time and setting of the play. Then he turns it over to the costume cutters. It's their responsibility to interpret the sketch in terms of fabric. Here is the result." Miss Timchuk paused dramatically in front of another door. "This is absolutely my favorite place. I used to work here when I was in college, and I felt just like a miser must feel when he knows his cellar is stuffed with money. Except I hoarded famous people."

Jenny was puzzled. "You did?"

Their guide invited them in. She began to stride up and down, snatching out costumes from the bulging racks.

"Well, look— " she said. "I had Henry the Eighth, and Anne Boleyn; Antony and Cleopatra; Julius Caesar! Kings and courtiers; saints and murderers." She pulled out a black cloak, muffled it up around her shoulders, and leered out at them as if she plotted their fiendish finish. Jenny laughed and reached out to touch some gold brocade.

"Do they ever use these costumes again?" she asked.

"No, except sometimes one may be torn apart, and the material used another season," Miss Timchuk said. "Or sometimes a costume may be brought out of storage and altered to fit someone else. Some might be aged, or glamorized. The rest are all kept."

"They must be very expensive." Jenny measured a length of burgundy velvet against her long legs.

"Yes, that one cost over a thousand dollars," she was told.

Dr. McNamara made a hasty notation in his notebook. "A thousand dollars! How long does it take to make a costume?" He gestured toward the overflowing racks.

Miss Timchuk thought about it. "For a simple design — say a peasant's costume — maybe a couple of days. Another, more elaborate design would take a week or so. It usually takes three fittings before the outfit is completed."

"What do you mean by 'aging' a costume?" Jenny asked.

"Sometimes the fabric is treated before the cutter works with it," Miss Timchuk told them, "but usually it is aged with paint or soot when the outfit is completed."

"We've always admired those colored sketches of the costume designs that they have for sale every year," Dr. McNamara commented. "My wife bought some, and we framed them for the hall."

"Yes, aren't they lovely?" she agreed. A boy, not much older than Toby and wearing curly sideburns, stuck his head inside the door and grinned.

"Hello there, Nicky. What are you doing here?" asked Miss Timchuk. "Shouldn't you be in class?"

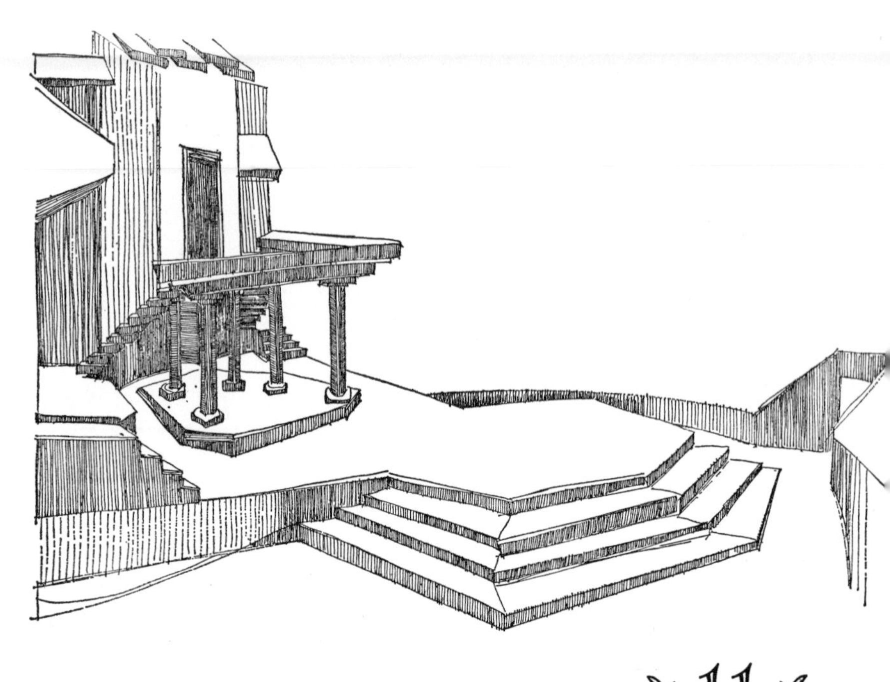

11

I LOST ONE of my boots last night. If you see it let me know." He waved and disappeared. Miss Timchuk shook her head.

"That was Nicky. He's one of our apprentices." She led them back down the corridor toward another room. A woman with bright pink cheeks signaled for them to enter.

"Hi, Charley," she said to their guide. "We're just redressing all the wigs for *The Tempest*." Her deft hands swabbed makeup from a hairpiece. "We do this after every performance," she told the visitors.

"Goodness, how many wigs do you have up there?"

Jenny asked, looking at the stacks of boxes piled high on the shelves.

"Oh, hundreds." Miss Timchuk ran despairing hands through her own ginger mop. "I'm going to kidnap a couple of them one of these dark nights." She whipped an elaborate blond creation from its block and perched it precariously on her bangs. Then she exchanged this for a glistening tower of black braids.

"This could have belonged to the Dark Lady of the Sonnets," she remarked.

Dr. McNamara beamed admiringly. "It could have, indeed."

"Who was she?" Jenny asked.

"Nobody knows." Miss Timchuk sighed, and replaced the wig. "Nobody knows a lot about Shakespeare. But he loved her somewhere and sometime. I guess that's all we really need to know."

The professor's pencil was poised. "Are all these wigs made in Canada?" he asked the pink-cheeked lady.

"No. They come from England. They're practically finished when they arrive, but our staff must trim and style them."

"And are they expensive?"

"Oh, gracious, yes. Each one costs over a hundred dollars."

Jenny's father rubbed his balding forehead. "You wouldn't have any odds and ends lying around, would you?" he asked. "I could use a small fringe."

"It must be hard work to style a wig." Jenny spoke to a young assistant. "I hate to fuss with my hair."

"Well, it does take patience." The girl stroked some smooth brown ringlets in her hand. "Our staff has considerable knowledge of the hairstyles of the period they must represent. The designer gives us a sketch of what he would like, and then we style it."

"Does that take a long time?"

"Oh, for some only a few hours. But for most it's a matter of days."

Dr. McNamara asked if the wigs could be used again in another production.

"Certainly." The lady with the pink cheeks spoke up. "We use them from season to season. Of course there may have to be alterations according to what the designer might require the next time."

"Thank you, ladies," said Miss Timchuk. "We know how busy you are." She motioned for Jenny and her father to follow her back into the corridor.

"Would you like to see one of the dressing rooms?" she asked.

"Yes, please!" Jenny looked into a cozy cubicle. Lightbulbs glowed above a long row of mirrors, and between the mirrors. On the dressing table was a collection of tissues and cold cream, bottles of rubbing alcohol and mineral oil, and a series of green metal containers.

"Those look like tackle boxes," said her father.

"They are!" Charlene Timchuk opened one of the makeup kits to show them the colored tubes of greasepaint. "Our actors have discovered that they're cheap and convenient and almost indestructible." She showed them a clothes rack where the current costumes were hung, and large labeled boxes underneath where the footwear was stored. Hats, lovely as bouquets, blossomed on an overhead rack.

They moved down the hall, and she opened another door.

"We have a few private dressing rooms. This one belongs to Miss Fitzsimmons, the Irish actress who is our guest star this season." Jenny inhaled, and Miss Timchuk sniffed and rolled up her eyes. "Doesn't it smell marvelous in here? She uses such heavenly perfume."

In the distance they heard great rollicking laughter.

"That's Miss Fitzsimmons. She's with her understudy onstage. We haven't seen the properties room yet, have we?"

They trotted after her.

"You ought to see this workshop before the season opens. It looks like a battlefield with all the armor lying around."

"Are all the properties made here?"

"Practically everything. We have professional carpenters who do all the wooden furniture and things like that. We make plastic and fiberglass armor . . . dishes . . . even flowers and fruit."

She opened a cupboard and took out a frightful bundle.

"Here's something we used in *Henry the Sixth*."

She held out a hideous severed head. Jenny made a small, sick sound.

"Don't be frightened. He isn't real." Cheerfully she tweaked Suffolk's bloody nose, and popped him back into storage. "Have you seen *The Tempest* yet?"

"Not yet."

"Just wait until you see what they've created for the banquet scene. If you like seafood I'll have to restrain you. Why don't we take a break now while we're waiting to get onstage?"

Back in the Green Room, Miss Timchuk introduced them to an assistant director and the fencing instructor, who were relaxing over a cup of coffee. While her father asked questions and took more notes Jenny slipped away to stare through a glass door into the lounge beyond. Nicky was there, talking with a group of young people. They all broke into loud laughter, and the meeting ended. As Nicky came out Miss Timchuk called him over to their table and introduced them.

"I found my boot," he said. "Toby had it mixed up with one of his."

"This is his first year at Stratford," she told them. "He's a university student who auditioned last fall and became one of our apprentices. There are about fifteen of them this year. It's a long day for you, isn't it, Nicky?"

"Well, early in the morning we study voice and take movement lessons from one of the older actors," he told them. "We've studied fencing, too . . ." he nodded in the direction of the instructor. "As a class we get together and act out scenes from a variety of plays . . . Christopher Fry or Samuel Beckett . . . Edward Albee, for instance. I'm an understudy for a couple of roles, and so we have rehearsals for that. Then we try and help out in the other departments if we're needed."

"You're also onstage part of the time," Miss Timchuk reminded him.

His smile was impish. "This year a peasant, but next year, *Macbeth!*"

"Not if you keep losing your boots." After he had gone she suggested that they have a look at the stage.

Jenny was allowed to run up the stairs leading to the roof of the portico. She dangled her legs over the edge and gazed out into the empty amphitheatre, wondering how it would feel to have two thousand pairs of critical eyes upon her. A little dizzy just thinking about it, she got up and made a demure bow to her invisible audience.

Miss Timchuk pointed across to the opposite side of the house.

"Do you see the central control booth over there?" she asked. "That's where the stage manager is positioned. He can see every aspect of the performance, and he can communicate with any part of the theatre, either by telephone or a light cue."

"Where is the electrician located?" Jenny's father had worn his pencil down.

"Oh, he's there, too. He operates the stage lights

from that position." She cupped a large hand around her mouth, and whispered confidentially, "That lighting booth cost twenty thousand dollars. What do you think of that?"

Jenny was impressed. "That's a lot of lightbulbs," she said.

Miss Timchuk showed them the orchestra loft where music was deflected into the auditorium by a specially designed acoustic ceiling. Up here also was the vast rehearsal loft. On their way back she paused backstage to show them the props for the matinee performance of *The Tempest*. A fantastic banquet had been created out of fruit, feathers and flowers. One platter was particularly tempting — a pyramid of scarlet lobster piled on bursting bunches of purple grapes. It looked so real that Jenny's mouth watered.

Jenny agreed with Mrs. Dumphrie that the theatre was a strange world. But it was something else — a fascinating beehive where intelligence, skill and talent combined to produce a special kind of fantasy. She was glad she had been allowed to look inside.

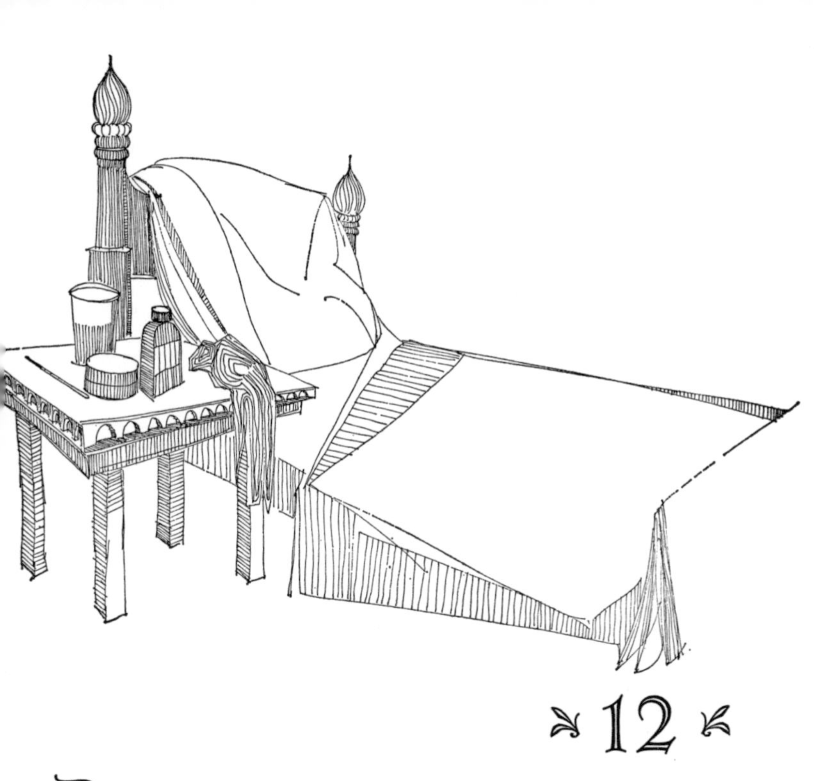

12

BY AFTERNOON a soggy layer of clouds had wrung out a dark curtain of rain over Stratford. As Jenny started off for the Kaplans' she bumped into Humphrey at the bottom of the stairs. He looked very pleased with himself.

"I said it would rain," he said. "My petunias needed it."

He proudly regarded the pair of metal swans, painted white, which decorated each side of the porch steps. Jenny found it hard to avoid swans. In one form or another she met them all over the city. These had swollen middles, bulging with red and white flowers. More petunias wept along the front walk and swam beside the driveway. Jenny hesitated before plunging into the watery world.

"The toaster isn't working, Humphrey."

"I fixed it once."

"Some morning my mother is going to strangle it with that worn-out electric cord," she promised him fiendishly.

He followed her out on the damp porch.

"I suppose you're going over to see that crazy family on Queen Street," he muttered.

"If you mean the Cardiffs . . . as a matter of fact, I'm not."

"They're queer. You shouldn't get mixed up with them."

"How do you know I am mixed up with them?"

He ignored the question. "You ought to watch your step," he advised her. "They're not decent people."

"Humphrey," she said pleasantly, "I think you'd better go and listen to the weather report."

"Just watch your step, that's all I have to say." He advanced to repeat himself, and his big feet in sloppy slippers skidded on the wet boards. Thunderously he went down. His head cracked against one of the metal swans, and a bonnet of petunias dangled over one eye. His fat legs struggled.

"I'll watch my step," Jenny said, offering him her hand to help him up, "and you watch yours, Humphrey." She left him mournfully sitting in his rocking chair.

Jenny felt quite at home as she sloshed through the streaming streets of Stratford. The river was deserted, and she wondered where the birds went in bad weather. The Kaplans had rented rooms in a pleasant tourist home on Cobourg Street. Mrs. Kaplan greeted her kindly, and almost pulled her up the stairs.

"Sarah will be very happy to have a visitor," she said. "It's hard to keep her in bed."

Mr. Kaplan, his bald head bent over a detective novel, sat like a sentry on a chair outside Sarah's room. He bobbed his head at Jenny, and shyly blinked his eyes.

"Poor darling," Mrs. Kaplan sighed, opening the door. She dawdled by the side of the bed, fussed with the sheets, and patted Sarah's cheek.

"Have a nice visit, girls. Daddy is just outside if you need anything."

"Tell him he doesn't have to keep watch," Sarah implored her. "I'll be all right soon. It's only an upset stomach."

"It makes him feel useful," whispered Mrs. Kaplan. She backed out of the bedroom and softly closed the door.

"It makes me feel foolish to be sick," Sarah said. Warily the two girls looked each other over.

Finally Jenny said, "It would be fun to live in New York City. I'd like to go there someday. I'd like to go up in one of those skyscrapers."

Sarah groaned and clutched the blanket. "Not me. I get nauseous."

"I'm going to be a skydiver when I grow up," Jenny told her.

"Jump out of an airplane!" Sarah struggled to sit up. She stared in admiration. "You must be terribly brave."

Jenny plumped the pillows for her, and Sarah leaned back. "I want to be a costume designer," she said, "but my mother has other plans for me."

"Almost everyone I've met since we arrived seems to be connected with the theatre in one way or another."

"Well, Papa isn't. He hates it!"

"Then why does he come?"

"Mama makes him. He's a dress designer on Seventh Avenue in the city. He makes plumpish clothes . . . for women about Mama's size. He calls them Kaplan's Klassics."

"That's a nice name."

"Every year at vacation time we come to Stratford to see the Festival. But my father makes the best of it. Whenever I see Mama wearing a dress that reminds me of Hamlet's mother, I figure he's picked up a few ideas."

"Your mother likes the theatre a lot?"

"Like it! She's the world's most frustrated actress." Sarah's smile was gay. "Mama was no Desdemona, of course, but she played the part of Molly Murphy, Professional Wrestler, on TV for a few years. Then I came along and really jinxed her career. First it was colic, and then my tonsils, and finally an emergency appendectomy. Now she's decided that I have to carry on the old show biz tradition."

"As an actress?"

Sarah picked up a hand mirror from the bedside table and made a face at herself.

"Isn't it a crime?" she asked. "With that face . . . and my Bronx brogue?" She put the mirror down. "She does have a second choice. I study both clarinet and flute. Someday she'd like me to play for the New York Philharmonic."

"I wish you'd been with me at the theatre this morning." Jenny described her backstage visit, and told Sarah all she remembered about the costumes. Sarah was an eager listener. But then Jenny's face grew serious.

"But something else is going on in this place. Strange things keep happening," she said. She told Sarah about the Cardiff family, and what Toby had said.

Sarah looked annoyed. "I hate to leave. It's like missing the end of a good movie."

"Do you have to go soon?"

"Next week. I have to miss *Don Giovanni* tonight, and I'm furious. I adore opera."

"Isn't that playing at the downtown theatre — the Avon?"

"Yes. The same actors often perform in both places, you know."

"I wish you could stay longer," Jenny said. "The Cardiffs are going to put on a puppet show, and they've asked me to help. I didn't think it would be much fun, but if you . . ."

Mrs. Kaplan bustled in.

"I hate to spoil your visit, girls, but Mrs. McNamara just called. She thinks that Jenny ought to come home."

"Is something wrong, Mrs. Kaplan?"

"I don't think so. She mentioned that a relative had arrived. A Cousin Cleo?"

13

IT WAS several years since Jenny had seen her cousin, but she remembered her as a very tall, very wiry old lady with an agonizing handclasp and a talent for criticism. When Dr. McNamara was a little boy and lost his mother, Cousin Cleo had taken him in hand and raised him. She was proud of the job she had done. She was not sure that Jenny's mother was doing her job as efficiently.

Jenny could hear voices from the living room as she came into the apartment. Her mother's voice was soft and low, and Miss McNamara's rose stridently above it. She took off her raincoat and pulled off her boots.

They made a great sucking sound. Then she went into the bathroom and looked at the drowned image of herself. Wet hair straggled over the collar of her blouse. She was sunburned and freckled. There just didn't seem to be much she could do about it. She took a deep breath and marched into the living room.

"Hello, Cousin Cleo."

"Well — Jennifer!"

Her relative sprang to her feet to make an inspection. She had a fiercely scrubbed red face and keen black eyes. Jenny was surprised to discover how much the lady had shrunk. Then she was seized, given a brisk kiss that was more of a bite, and her hands were gripped tightly. Cousin Cleo burst into tears.

Bewildered, Jenny appealed silently to her mother. Maggie McNamara only made soothing sounds, and patted their guest gently on the back.

"But she's so tall," gasped the old lady, mopping at her eyes, "so grown-up!" She assaulted her nose with a hanky, and then blew heartily. "The last time I saw Jennifer she was no higher than a doorknob . . . no thicker than a teaspoon!" This improbable memory brought on a fresh shower of tears. Jenny, who had been rained on outside, now found herself being rained on inside.

"Yes, she's a big girl," agreed Mrs. McNamara, still patting Cousin Cleo on the back as if she were a cranky baby.

Shaken, the lady tried to compose herself. She took a few appraising steps, and looked at Jenny from another angle. "When you decide to stop trying to look like a boy," she observed, "you just might make a very handsome girl."

Jenny was not sure this was meant to be a compliment. She smiled cautiously.

"Such big teeth!" Cousin Cleo stepped up to have a better look. "But when the rest of her grows up to fit them they'll do well enough."

Jenny clamped her mouth shut.

"Terribly scrawny, though. Her father was like that once, but I plumped him up."

Mrs. McNamara raised an eyebrow. "Indeed you did," she said.

"It's raisins before breakfast . . . that's what does it. Not *after* breakfast, mind you. Before." The inspector general paraded slowly around her victim. "She has the McNamara feet," she sighed. "I always said that if the McNamaras didn't turn so much growth into their shoes they'd be regular giants."

Jenny's mother was very pleasant. "Yes, you've always said that."

"Straighten up, Jennifer," finished the old lady. "Eat raisins. Don't squint. Stand tall. Sit down."

Not sure she could do all of these things at the same time, Jenny compromised by kneeling awkwardly on the floor and tucked her feet under her. Then their visitor embarked on a long recital of the trip east from British Columbia. There were McNamaras in every province who had extended great hospitality; there were operations to discuss, many of them in terrifying detail; there were many brilliant cousins to be mentioned. Jenny learned that her family tree bristled with baton-twirling experts, ornamental swimming stars and piano virtuosos. One clever young man had just won a national slogan contest and collected a year's supply of canned dog food.

"But Sydney doesn't *have* a dog," Jenny pointed out. "He's allergic to them."

Cousin Cleo was unfortunately vague on this point. Sydney was smart and lucky, and these were definitely McNamara traits.

"How long are you planning to be with us?" Jenny asked when Cousin Cleo paused to draw breath.

"I'm in no hurry at all," she was told. "I'll be here indefinitely."

"That's what I thought," said Jenny. Her smile felt sticky and insincere. A summer in Stratford seemed bad enough — but a summer in Stratford with Cousin Cleo was impossible. It was like living under a curfew, or having a lingering illness that wouldn't go away. She resolved that when she grew up she would marry another only child. That way her children would have a minimum of relatives. It would be the only humane thing to do.

At dinner, after an affectionate reunion between her father and his cousin, Jenny and her mother found themselves anchored outside the conversational waters. Miss McNamara had many memories to refresh. Everytime Jenny started to yawn she took a drink. She felt like a camel preparing for an extended desert trip. She sloshed. At last the telephone saved her from further torture. It was Toby, and she could tell he wanted to be friendly.

"The girls wondered if you could come over soon and help them with the puppet show."

"I don't know," she sighed. "Maybe I can get away, but don't count on it."

"What do you mean?"

"My cousin is here."

"Well, see what you can do. By the way — we have an unlisted telephone number now. I'll give it to you, if you like."

"All right." She marked it down beside the telephone. "Tell your sisters I'll try and come over in the morning. After I eat my raisins."

"After what?"

"Never mind. Thanks for calling, Toby."

Back at the dinner table her relative wanted to know who had called.

"Just a boy I know."

The old lady frowned. "You're entirely too young to be running around with boys."

"I don't run around with him. I just like him. Boys are just people," Jenny spoke up.

"He's a new friend, Cleo," Maggie McNamara said quietly. "His father is Alexander Cardiff, the Shakespearean actor."

"Oh, *him*."

"Why do you say it like that?" Jenny's ears felt hot.

"Because I've been reading an article about him. It

said that he thinks Stratford has one of the finest theatres in the world."

"What's wrong with that?" Mrs. McNamara's voice tasted of tartness. "I happen to agree with him."

"There's nothing wrong with it. I happen to agree with him, too," was the mild reply.

They all relaxed.

"In fact, this season I shall see everything," announced the old lady enthusiastically. "Even that new play by young whatsisname . . . the one where everyone wears masks like in Greek tragedy."

"Yes, it ought to be interesting, all right," Dr. McNamara agreed. "It opens at the Avon next week."

"I even intend to see the National Ballet Company," was the next surprising announcement.

"But you've never liked ballet," Mrs. McNamara remarked. "You've always said that ballet dancers reminded you of ostriches in bedroom slippers."

"Then maybe I've never seen a good ballet." Cousin Cleo was serious. "I've discovered that prejudice is a sign of old age — no matter how old you are. Maybe I'll learn something. But how I wish they would do another Gilbert and Sullivan operetta," she continued wistfully. "We used to see them when I was a girl. All that silliness — how we laughed!"

"I like them, too." The hostess cut another generous wedge of chocolate fudge cake, and handed it to their guest. A weakness for second helpings was also a McNamara trait.

"But you can't spend your life thinking about the

glories of the past," Cousin Cleo went on. "That's also a sign of old age, and I shall never be old. Think of all the wonderful things to come. Talented young people all over Canada are developing right now who hope to do such marvelous things. They'll write the exciting new plays, and they'll compose the strange new music of the future."

"That's true." Dr. McNamara lit up his pipe.

Jenny wondered where she fitted in.

"Challenge and conquest. That's what makes life an adventure at any age," Cousin Cleo proclaimed. She attacked her cake with strengthened appetite. Jenny found herself almost liking the old girl.

"We'll take a walk one of these days," she was told. "I want to see the Festival through my own eyes — and through yours, Jennifer."

14

WHEN JENNY came into the kitchen in the morning, her mother was holding a cup of coffee in one hand and a paperback book in the other.

"Is Cousin Cleo still asleep?" she whispered. Maggie McNamara's girlish laughter rang out.

"Good heavens, no! Cleo was up at six o'clock. She took a cold shower to improve her circulation and made a large pot of oatmeal. Then she went for a walk. She wanted to wake you up but I told her you were a growing girl and needed your rest."

"Oh thanks, Mother." Jenny dropped a grateful kiss and stretched hugely.

"But I expect she'll want you to go with her soon.

Your cousin is a great walker, you know. You'd better have some of that oatmeal and start getting into condition."

Jenny gingerly lifted the lid of the pot, hastily dropped it back into place and made a gagging sound.

"No, thank you," she said. "I just couldn't face all those lumps this early in the morning." She poured a large glass of fresh orange juice and drank noisily. When her mother returned to the book, Jenny took careful aim and hit the wall plaque with a seed.

"Stop that," said Mrs. McNamara without looking up.

"What are you reading?"

"I'm doing some homework. We'll be seeing *The Tempest* at a matinee this week, and I want to read the play again before we do."

"Will I like it?"

"I think so. It's full of magic. There's a shipwreck, and a monster, and of course romance."

"Well, at least the monster appeals to me. And there's a banquet, too. I almost ate the lobster."

"What are your plans for today?"

"I thought I'd see if Sarah is well enough to go out. I'd like to take her over to the Cardiffs' with me to see the puppets."

"You like Sarah after all?"

"Yes. I only wish she could stay in Stratford longer."

"What play are the girls planning to do?"

"Toby mentioned *Peter and the Wolf*."

"How lovely."

Jenny sighed. "I don't know the first thing about puppets. I wish I could get out of it."

"It might be fun, you know."

"It sounds so childish."

When she called at Sarah's tourist home Mrs. Kaplan was waving a thermometer.

"If Sarah's temperature is normal then we'll let her go out today," she promised.

Mr. Kaplan hovered nearby. When the thermometer was finally extracted from Sarah's jaws he and his wife gravely conferred.

"Normal," said Mr. Kaplan.

"Normal," said Mrs. Kaplan. They exchanged an anxious glance and read the thermometer again.

"Normal," they agreed.

"But it's *always* normal," Sarah told them. "I haven't had a temperature since I had the Asian flu in the fourth grade."

"One can't be too careful," Mrs. Kaplan said firmly. She gave Sarah a vitamin pill, a raincoat, and a warning. "Now take it easy, darling. Nothing strenuous."

The girls walked sedately down the block, and made a turn. Then Sarah gave a fierce whoop of release.

"I'll race you to the corner!" she shouted. They were both out of breath by the time they arrived at the Cardiffs'. Toby was busy in the back yard putting the finishing touches on a stage. Children of all ages stood watching, and when he tacked up blue velvet curtains with gold tassels they sent up a cheer.

Jenny was impressed. "It's beautiful, Toby." She introduced her new friend.

"Go ahead inside," Toby told them. "The girls are expecting you."

"Are you going to be in the show?" Jenny asked.

"Not me. Maybe I'll be stage manager."

Portia was at work on the drums. The whole house was shaking. From the living room, over the sound of the cuckoo clocks, came the determined voice of an operatic soprano on the record player. Hamlet, oblivious to everything, snoozed in his cage. Fat Falstaff, one of the cats, rubbed affectionately against their ankles. Pistol, the skinny one, gave a wild shriek and jumped from a cupboard to the top of the refrigerator.

"Olivia? Rosalind!" Jenny called.

Upstairs a rumpus raged. Footsteps thudded swiftly back and forth, and then a faint voice would stitch a protest through the racket.

Suddenly the violent eruptions beneath their feet stopped altogether. Shortly afterward a fat, red-cheeked girl burst into the kitchen. She headed straight for the kitchen sink and poured herself a large glass of water.

"Hi," she said between gulps. "Portia here."

Jenny and Sarah introduced themselves.

"Hard work. Thirsty. Go back now," the girl

gasped. She drained another glass of water. "Nobody here? Wait."

Portia threw back her head and uttered a blood-curdling jungle sound. It was very effective. The running footsteps overhead stopped and then tumbled toward the stairs. Portia nodded her head with satisfaction.

"Coming now. 'Bye."

The talking telegram disappeared down the cellar steps. Olivia, Rosalind and Viola, giggling and perspiring, fluttered into the kitchen in a cloud of feathers.

"We were having a pillow fight," Olivia said. "Have you seen the puppets yet?"

Rosalind dashed into the living room, and came out with her arms full of bodies. Mrs. Cardiff, smelling of carnations, drifted in after her. Her eyes had dark circles underneath, and she was pale.

"Mother's still upset about the other day," Rosalind whispered to Jenny.

"Here's Peter." Viola blew up her hair and slipped her arm into the cotton sleeve which was attached to the puppet's head. She bobbed his head in greeting. His cheeks were like two ripe strawberries, and he had a woolly cap of yellow yarn hair.

"And Cat." Olivia snatched up another. This was a snobbish-looking feline with an aristocratic nose and a wide stare.

"And my creation — Bird." Rosalind brought forward a puppet that looked like a feather duster. It had a huge beak and a topknot of red and green fuzz. It was silly and slightly cockeyed, and Jenny liked it best.

"Here's Wolf." Mrs. Cardiff made him show all his teeth. His green eyes gleamed above a nose which shone like a wet ripe olive.

"Don't forget Grandfather!" This was dignity with whiskers.

"Duck . . . and the hunters." All the puppets, still undressed, made a colorful company.

"Mother still has to do the costumes," Viola said.

"May I help?" Sarah begged. "I'd love to dress them."

"I have a whole bag of odds and ends," said Mrs. Cardiff. "Let's have a look, and see what we can find."

It was the happiest morning Jenny had spent in a long time. It was fun to be with gay young people. Sarah's quicksilver fingers ran through the bright scraps of cloth. She could drape and pin and sew with swiftness and precision. Peter soon grew splendid in a striped shirt and green jacket. Grandfather was impressive in a rough peasant smock. In the meantime the girls showed Jenny a script of the play.

"We want you to be the narrator," Olivia said. "Our voices are too light, and anyway we'll be busy manipulating the puppets."

"Will there be music?"

"*Peter and the Wolf* is music," Rosalind said. "For instance, Peter is represented by the strings. We only have one, of course. Mother plays the violin."

"Badly, I'm afraid," Mrs. Cardiff admitted. "My arm wobbles."

"Let's not forget Portia," Viola reminded them. "Her drums have to represent the hunters and their guns."

"I sort of play an oboe," Jenny offered, "if you need one."

"Good. Duck is an oboe."

"We also need a French horn," said Rosalind. "Does anybody know a French horn?"

Nobody did.

"How about a flute or clarinet for Bird and Cat?"

"I play both!" Sarah's little eyes shone. Then she frowned. "I forgot. I have to go home next week. But I can fill in until you find somebody else."

"We need a bassoon." Olivia was stumped. "I don't know where we'll ever find one of those. Maybe Sybilla knows someone."

"Sybilla *is* a bassoon," Rosalind said dryly. "She wouldn't even need an instrument with that voice of hers."

"I can't be the narrator," Jenny said hesitantly. "I haven't had any theatrical experience at all. Once we had a school play, but all I had to do was grow."

They stared.

"I was a stalk of corn. I was supposed to ripen when the sun shone. Somebody watered my head with a watering can, and I caught an awful cold."

Everybody laughed. Portia, dolphin-like, surfaced again.

"Lunch, please," she demanded. "Hungry!"

"Is it time?" Sarah asked. With a multitude of clicks and chirps every clock in the house sounded the hour.

"It's time," Mrs. Cardiff said. "Why don't you girls stay and eat with us? I'll call your parents."

Even making lunch was fun. Olivia whacked off thick slices from a crusty loaf of bread while Jenny cut uneven slices of ham. Rosalind painted on bright patches of mustard. Toby, coming in from outside, decided he would eat in the back yard.

"That's a wonderful idea," agreed Viola. "We'll all go outside."

Loaded with sandwiches and lemonade, cups, plates and paper napkins, they followed him into the hot, flower-scented afternoon. The neighborhood children retreated respectfully beyond the fence and then dangled over it to watch. While they ate, Jenny glanced through her copy of *Peter and the Wolf*.

"Why don't you read it to us?" Mrs. Cardiff suggested easily.

"I can't," Jenny said. "I'm too embarrassed."

"Please. We'd like very much to hear it."

Jenny began to read. Her tongue felt clumsy. It tripped over words which reared like boulders in its path.

"I can't do it." Jenny was miserable. "You'll have to find somebody else."

"I like your voice," Rosalind said confidently. "It's so deep and strong. Try again, Jenny."

Encouraged, she took a new breath. The words suddenly seemed more flexible. Feeling a sense of power, she charged along and realized that she was actually enjoying herself. When the story stopped for musical effects the girls supplied comical imitations. When she finished, everyone looked at her with delight. There was a spatter of applause from beyond the fence. Mrs. Cardiff warmly took hold of Jenny's hands.

"You're good," she said. "You have a certain quality, Jenny. I think you may have the makings of an actress."

"Me?"

"Yes, you. Now let's try it again."

15

THERE were bright and busy days. Mornings Sarah and Jenny rehearsed for the puppet show or went swimming in the Lions Club pool. When Toby was free he gave Jenny her first fencing lessons and taught her all the movements of his role in *Henry the Fifth*. On the afternoon she was to see *The Tempest*, he took her backstage before the performance and introduced her to the director — a nervous man on elastic legs who bounced all over the theatre with his hair standing on end. He was Welsh, with an unpronounceable name, but everyone called him Max. Toby seemed in such awe of him that Jenny asked what it was he did.

"A director?" Toby generated a special excitement.

"He's the master technician — the one who pulls all the talent together and sets it in motion." Miss Timchuk hurried past with a group of panting Japanese dignitaries. She waved.

"The director uses people to create a pattern onstage," Toby explained carefully, "that will interpret the meaning of the play in the fullest and most artistic sense. It's what I want to do someday."

The Tempest captivated her. In the opening shipwreck scene she watched a wave of actors move their bodies like a battering wall of water. Wailing sound effects and dramatic lighting added to the violent impression of a storm at sea. The sight of a great ship straining and cracking was so powerful that Jenny tore her program into a snowstorm. During the whole play she was conscious of the director's shaping hand. Out of printed words he had helped create this fantastic province, as airy and beautiful as music on the wind.

She was discussing it with her mother the next morning when Cousin Cleo caught her at the breakfast table.

"Today we shall see the exhibits, Jennifer," she announced.

"But I promised the Cardiff girls . . ."

"You'll enjoy it," her mother promised. "By the way, if you run into Humphrey on your way out, would you tell him I'd like to see him."

Humphrey was sitting wedged in his rocking chair, staring blankly at his petunias. Cousin Cleo stopped.

"What do you do?" she demanded.

Surprised, he blinked round eyes and stared.

"I asked you a question," said Miss McNamara irritably. "I asked you what you did."

Jenny felt sorry for him. "Sometimes he delivers milk," she told her cousin. "And he invents things, too."

Humphrey ignored them both and studied his stumpy fingernails. "I'm a landlord," he said.

"A landlord!" repeated Cousin Cleo grandly. She folded her wiry arms and fixed him with a glittering eye. "Then may I suggest, Mr. Dumphrie, that you administer first aid at once to Mrs. McNamara's refrigerator. It gasped and expired sometime during the night."

"Not my fault," he mumbled, "if people don't take care of things."

"Impudence." Cousin Cleo carried a bulging handbag that had been made from the hide of an unlucky baby alligator. She took a poke at Humphrey with the tiny but ferocious snout. "Out of that chair," she ordered. "Stand up when a lady speaks to you." But Humphrey was stuck tight. Jenny tried to help him in his panicky struggle to free himself, but when he managed to get to his feet the chair was still fastened behind, as snug as a bustle.

"Impudence!" Miss McNamara said once again, and flounced down the porch steps. Her walking shoes made explosive sounds as they hit the pavement. She scribbled off down the street like a runaway pencil, and Jenny hurried to catch up.

"Look, Jennifer! A horse-drawn milk wagon. I didn't know they still existed."

Jenny stroked the soft nose of the big Clydesdale horse as she passed, and he rudely blew out his lips at her. As they approached Exhibition Hall her cousin suddenly changed her mind.

"Let's visit the island first. It's one of my favorite places," she said. In the distance, crouched at the water's edge, Jenny caught sight of Evan Montmorency. She hadn't seen him since the morning she and Toby had watched him feed the swans. She told her cousin about him as they crossed the humpbacked bridge. He looked very frail in a light shirt and ragged trousers. He was sketching some Canada geese that paddled nearby.

"Mr. Montmorency," she called. "I'd like you to meet another admirer. This is my cousin, Miss McNamara."

"I'm very pleased to see you, sir." The sharp voice of the maiden lady was suddenly softer and warmer. "And very surprised to find you here. You should still be on the stage. Jenny tells me you've retired, and I'm sorry to hear it."

Slowly the actor straightened up. His drawn face was uncertain. "Oh, yes," he said. "Yes, I'm very much retired."

"Well, you shouldn't be," she reprimanded him. "You've let us down, that's what you've done."

"Have I?"

"Of course. Some of these up-and-coming young people could learn a great deal from a man like Evan Montmorency. Besides — I don't think idleness agrees with you. You're too thin, man. When was the last time you had a decent meal?"

He replied simply: "I can't remember."

"Then we'll expect you for dinner tonight." Cousin Cleo rummaged briskly through the baby alligator and found a pencil and some paper. She wrote their address, folded the paper firmly, and tucked it into his shirt pocket. Then she gave him an administrative nudge on the chest.

"Put on some decent clothes, and be on time. Six-thirty."

"But I don't think — "

"Don't think anything," she scolded. "Just come." She looked into his troubled eyes and placed her scrawny hand on his arm. "We'll be honored to have you, Mr. Montmorency. We truly will."

Miss McNamara bolted off, and once again Jenny scrambled to catch up. The old lady was down on her knees examining the soil and condition of the flower beds. Happily she sniffed the fragrant sunshine.

"I wish you hadn't said that — about wearing decent clothes," Jenny said softly. "I don't think he has any."

"When a man loses interest in how he looks, then someone has to take an interest for him," her cousin said firmly. "He'll find something respectable to put on his back — don't worry about that. And he'll bring flowers. He's a gentleman, Jenny. Wait and see."

She popped back on her feet, and started toward the bridge.

"Something bothers me," Jenny confided. "Olivia said that Mr. Montmorency asked her father to get him work at Stratford a few years ago. She said that Mr. Cardiff knew it was hopeless. By then Mr. Montmorency couldn't remember stage directions, or even his lines any more. He did arrange an audition, out of kindness, I guess. When they told the old man that they couldn't use him he stopped coming to see the Cardiffs. Olivia thinks he still blames her father, and Toby thinks . . ." She paused, reluctant to finish.

"I think for a long-legged girl you're mighty short of wind," hurled Miss McNamara over her shoulder. Jenny quickened her pace and glanced back toward the island. Following them in the distance was the figure of the aged actor.

16

AS THEY WENT into Exhibition Hall a pretty young girl handed them some literature about the Festival activities. It was still early in the day. The hall was cool, quiet and almost empty. Just inside the door a rustic swing had been set up on display. It was entwined with vines and flowers — so lifelike that Jenny touched them to make sure they weren't actually growing there. Seated, with little hands just touching the ropes as if she waited for a push, was a mannequin. Her head was tilted and her lips were parted as if she were about to sing.

"It's Olivia!" Rapturously Cousin Cleo clasped her hands. "She looked just like that in *Twelfth Night* last season. See the exquisite embroidery on her bodice, Jennifer."

Jenny stood in silence and looked at the tableau. She had long ago outgrown her dolls, but the costumed figure brought back to her the pleasure she had once taken in them.

"Look, here she is again — wearing the same black velvet outfit." Miss McNamara pointed to the wall which was covered with sketches from previous productions. Jenny wondered if Mr. Kaplan's blinking eyes had photographed the graceful designs yet. Her cousin nudged her along, eagerly pointing out things to her. Jenny suggested that they separate and meet later.

Relieved to be alone, she slipped around a corner and found herself in a section devoted to children's books. For a while she browsed among all the volumes until she discovered the special display of Canadian authors. Each bright and shiny book jacket seemed to be one tiny interlocking part in the great jigsaw puzzle which was Canada. There were stories of Eskimo and Indian life, adventures of the early explorers and pioneers, tales of rural Quebec villages, eastern fishing ports and prairie farms. All the gay pictures and printed words represented the history of her sprawling native land. Intrigued, she settled down and lost herself in them. It was a long time later when she became aware of angry sounds, like persistent buzzing flies.

"And I say it's nonsense," rasped the familiar voice

of Cousin Cleo. "If he thinks Sir Francis Bacon wrote the plays of William Shakespeare then that's his privilege. There's never been a shortage of fools in this world. But he'll never convince me."

"I only suggested that you read his book and examine his evidence." This was a reedy voice Jenny had heard before.

"Evidence? Pipe dreams, you mean! I know all about you anti-Stratfordians. You sniff about like bad-mannered beagles and keep trying to knock poor William off his pedestal. Just because he died a solid and respectable citizen doesn't mean he wasn't bright, you know."

"The fact is — " replied the tremulous male voice, "your William Shakespeare was the son of a butcher."

"Glover," interrupted Cousin Cleo.

"Who attended a dreary little village grammar school."

"And a very good it was for the day," she broke in testily.

"He was raised a provincial, educated a provincial, and died a provincial."

"Died a genius," she corrected him.

"My dear lady. Can you accept the notion that the Divine Bard — author of the ecstatic *Antony and Cleopatra* — was practically raised on a dunghill in Stratford-upon-Avon?"

Jenny heard her cousin draw an outraged breath, as if she had just been skewered. She peeked around the shelves to witness the verbal battle. The opponents had drawn themselves up like bristling birds ready for combat. The man was spindly and potbellied, but for a little stove he generated a powerful amount of heat. Jenny recognized Mr. Smallwood. He was trying to press a book upon Miss McNamara, who was determined that she would not take it.

"Yes, I can accept that fact," she said. "Because country imagery shines out of every play. They couldn't have been written by anyone other than the boy who grew up beside the Avon — who knew every wildflower that grew there. Even *Antony and Cleopatra* has cows in it. What did Sir Francis Bacon know about cows, I ask you?"

Now her opponent changed his tactics. He replaced the offensive volume on the shelf and attempted to be patient.

"All I say," he went on quietly, "is that it seems more reasonable that someone better educated, more experienced and more . . . sophisticated, let us say . . . wrote what we now call the Shakespearean plays. Perhaps a member of the aristocracy, who for a very good reason only *borrowed* the name William Shakespeare."

"Then you don't know a thing about writers," Cousin Cleo said flatly. "Who would be such an idiot as to let another man take all the credit for four hundred years?"

Mr. Smallwood broke out into a dew of perspiration. He snatched back the volume from the shelf and began to thumb rapidly through it. "A member of the nobility wouldn't want his own name publicly associated with the stage," he explained. "This author points out that it wasn't considered a respectable occupation for an aristocrat." He gave a deep sigh. "Of course, he didn't know then that his plays would still be popular now."

"Shakespeare knew it. Even in his early sonnets he said he would be immortal."

"But this author proposes many men better qualified to have written the plays. Sir Francis Bacon, of course, is a leading contender. And what of Christopher Marlowe?"

"Don't mention him to me!" Cousin Cleo said fiercely. "You add insult to injury. Marlowe was killed in a drunken brawl. Everyone knows Shakespeare was a temperate man. Really!"

"I have in my possession," Mr. Smallwood whispered mysteriously, "certain secret papers which prove conclusively that William Shakespeare was a fraud."

"Nonsense."

Jenny decided that it was time to dash some water on the bonfire. She came around the corner of the bookshelves.

"I didn't know there was all this mystery about William Shakespeare," she said.

"There needn't be," said her cousin, "if so-called scholars would stop trying to muddy up plain truths. They can't even decide among themselves how Shakespeare looked."

"Nobody knows for certain how he *did* look," sputtered Mr. Smallwood. He wiped his forehead.

"Well, I do." Miss McNamara skimmed along a row of books, and stopped to wrench out another large volume. She pointed to the engraving on the outer jacket. It was a mild-looking man without much hair. "There he is."

Mr. Smallwood shook his head angrily. "That's the Droeshout engraving," he scoffed. "It was used as frontispiece to the First Folio of Shakespeare's plays when it was published in sixteen twenty-three. He'd been dead at least seven years."

"When I've been dead for seven years," was her prompt retort, "I certainly expect someone will remember how I looked."

"I assure you, madam," he said grimly, "that the memory of your face will be imprinted in my mind *forever*." He chose another book and tapped the cover. "This is a picture of the life-sized bust by Geraert Janssen which his family purchased for Shakespeare's tomb. I'm sure they paid handsomely for it. Shakespeare probably knew Mr. Janssen personally. I conclude it is the more accurate representation."

This was another peaceful face — too serene to be the object of such passionate dispute. Jenny smiled.

"I like mysteries," she said. "I want to know more about this man William Shakespeare."

"To understand any man you must first understand the climate of his age," the intense man urged kindly.

"Learn for yourself about Elizabethan England. What did the people eat and wear and read? What were their politics and their amusements? Who were their enemies? It's fascinating stuff."

Cousin Cleo nodded in agreement. "Exactly," she said. Bending companionably over the books, the two figures engaged in a more subdued conversation. Jenny left them together. The hall suddenly seemed stuffy, and her head was aching. She went back for one last look at the figure on the swing.

Olivia was a sight. Red streaks smeared her pale cheeks and stained the frosty points of lace on her bodice. The deep folds of her skirt held pockets of ketchup-colored paint. There was a steady drip, drip, drip as a pool as dark as blood widened on the floor.

The young girl who had taken their admissions was coming back to her post with a cup of coffee in her hand. She stopped in shock. Someone had even given Olivia the push she had been waiting for. As they watched, her figure slowly toppled off the swing.

17

THE FIRST THING Maggie McNamara did when she learned she was to have a dinner guest that evening was to go out and buy a magnificent roast of beef. Then she spent the afternoon closeted in the kitchen making a great racket with the inadequate equipment. Humphrey had come earlier, given the refrigerator a few blows from the side and a kick from behind, and started it running again. Jenny and Cousin Cleo were careful not to get in the way. They straightened the apartment and put an extra leaf in the dining room table. They set it up with candlesticks and an old tablecloth that was as fine and delicate as cobwebs.

Miss McNamara then put on her best dark dress,

placed two coins of color high on her cheeks, and poured a large quantity of strong lemony scent on herself. In spite of these preparations, and even the warm rich sizzle of the meat, Jenny felt nervous and upset. The morning had ended so strangely, and the afternoon edition of the *Beacon Herald* had carried only a brief account of the vandalism at the *Twelfth Night* exhibit. She also worried about Evan Montmorency. What if he arrived in some outlandish costume? What if he failed to come at all?

"I don't think he'll turn up," she whispered around the kitchen door. "Cousin Cleo kind of browbeat him into it."

"Stop worrying." Her mother came out to put her arms around Jenny and to give her a quick hug. "We know that you're fond of the old fellow, honey. Just trust us. We'll take care of him."

Her father came in and went singing to the shower. It was good to hear all the busy welcoming sounds. Then there was a gentle rapping at the door. Relieved, Jenny flew to open it. It was Dylan Forde who stood there, twisting his tiny hands together.

"Is your mother busy?" he appealed. "The most dreadful thing has happened."

"What is it, Mr. Forde?"

"Disaster, that's all."

"Disaster?" She waited anxiously.

He explained. "I invited Sybilla to dinner. I wanted to prove I could do something by myself. I cooked a cheese soufflé that was a vision — a masterpiece!"

"But what happened?"

"It fell. The wretched girl was late, and so my soufflé fell. It was taller than a chef's cap, but they don't wait forever, you know. She spoiled it all."

"I'm so sorry," Jenny told him. "Maybe Mother can help."

"I have to borrow a can of something. Anything. Pork and beans will do, and it's better than she deserves."

"Pork and beans indeed!" Mrs. McNamara, all in blue, came forward. "You'll eat with us. We're having a dinner guest, and I'm sure he will be delighted to meet you both."

Dylan Forde retreated. "Absolutely not," he protested. "I wouldn't dream of imposing."

There was another knock — this time a very loud one. Then the door burst open, and there was Sybilla, smiling brilliantly.

"I knew I heard your voice," she told Dylan. "And here I am — just famished." She glowed at them, but her host had frozen solid.

"What did you cook for me?" she coaxed. "I can't wait to see it."

"It *was* a soufflé."

"But I adore soufflé." She threw warm arms around him and pinched his cheeks.

"Well, it's too late. You never are on time, Sybilla. The whole thing is ruined."

She was very beautiful as she stared at him with

stricken eyes. Her long gown was the color of fire. Dark hair gleamed over her bare shoulders.

"Never mind." Maggie McNamara began to laugh. "I've just asked Mr. Forde to allow you to eat dinner with us. He's refused, but I think you can persuade him."

"Refused?" gasped the folksinger. "He ruins my dinner — and refuses to let me eat anywhere else?" She flickered into the living room like a flame. "I shall adore having dinner with you. If Dylan won't come, then let him go scramble an egg."

Jenny dashed off to set two extra places while her mother took Dylan's resisting arm and tried to make him feel at home. Cousin Cleo, standing a safe distance from their unexpected guests, stared suspiciously as if she thought there was some danger she might be singed. It looked as if it would be an interesting evening even if the guest of honor never did arrive. But exactly at six-thirty he presented himself.

He made a striking appearance. Jenny wondered where he had found the set of evening clothes. His silver hair was perfectly brushed, his trousers sharp, his shoes gleaming. He carried a large paper of long-stemmed roses which he gravely presented to Mrs. McNamara. For Cousin Cleo and Jenny there were two perfect buds. Jenny went shy with pleasure and surprise.

The conversation, which had been chiefly confined to Sybilla's corner of the living room, started up with the sprightliness of a Sousa march. Everyone was interested in the distinguished old man who had arrived so jauntily to enhance the party. There was also much comment on the morning's paint episode. Dylan Forde and Evan Montmorency had little to say on the matter, but Miss McNamara was never reticent with her opinions.

"It was young hoodlums," she decided. "The country is just overrun with them these days. They don't work. They won't go to school. All they know is how to make mischief."

"This looks like more than mischief, Cleo," Dr. McNamara put in thoughtfully. "All these separate bits and pieces of vandalism add up to something more than that."

"Young people only comprehend violence," his relative persisted. "They don't understand the meaning of decency or beauty."

"But the other night you said that young people — " Jenny began.

"I said that some would grow up to greatness. But what about the rest? Why can't they appreciate the finer things now?"

"But so many of them do!" Sybilla spoke emphatically. "Don't you know that thousands of students come here every year? I've seen them hike into town like pilgrims, with bedrolls on their back. I've seen them wait in line for hours just to buy tickets. And in the final weeks of the season they come in busloads for special performances from all over Canada and the United States."

Now Dylan Forde spoke up. "And you should see how much they appreciate the plays — you should listen to their reactions, and hear their questions and comments when the performance is over. Sometimes their perceptions are so acute it's almost frightening. They respond. They're alive! As far as I'm concerned they're marvelous."

"Why, Dylan," Sybilla said, gripping his hand, "I didn't know you felt like that."

"Dinner," announced the hostess, making a mock curtsy like a theatrical maid, "is served."

"Tonight Mr. Montmorency must be surrounded by youth and beauty," Sybilla exclaimed, taking charge. "Jenny shall sit to his left, and I shall sit to his right."

Cousin Cleo gave an outraged snort and stomped over to sit down beside Dylan Forde. From there she sent hostile glances in the direction of the lovely young woman who had already spoiled her digestion. Sybilla, cheered by the quick arrival of a loaded dinner plate, was successfully silenced for the next twenty minutes.

"Why Mr. Montmorency," Jenny's mother said as she served him, "you've hurt your hand."

He laughed. "No, that's only a little paint. I was working with oils this afternoon. It seems to relax me."

It had been like a scene from a play. The leaping candlelight, pure linen and animated faces of her family and friends had seemed strange and lovely to

Jenny. Dr. McNamara gaily splashing wine into crystal glasses; the adult laughter spilling over; the mahogany sound of the old man's voice as he wove amusing stories for them out of the fabric of his past. But she was suddenly depressed. A tiny smear of red paint had spoiled it all. She thought of the ruined exhibit in Exhibition Hall. Then she thought of Toby and what he had said about Evan Montmorency.

Sybilla finally put down her knife and fork, patted her lips with a napkin, and spoke. "You must write your memoirs, sir."

"I'm not a writer, young lady," the actor told her. "I'm not much of anything, I'm afraid. But I've been jotting down notes for years. Someday, perhaps, I will do something with them."

"Not someday," she insisted. "Now. It will make a fascinating book. Your memories are full of color and humor . . . and all those famous names we've heard of all our lives."

The professor leaned forward. "You're right, Sybilla," he said. "It *would* make an interesting book."

Cousin Cleo, sitting dismally out of the limelight, perked up immediately. "I was just about to suggest it myself." She frowned at Sybilla. "And I'm just the one who can help."

"In what way, Cleo?"

"I'll use my tape recorder. Mr. Montmorency and I will chat together about his experiences, and I'll record our conversations. Then we'll organize, write, and publish. We'll make a fortune."

"I don't know about making a fortune," Dr. McNamara grinned, "but you'll make a fine team. It's a good project."

In spite of his interest the old man had tired. His confident manner and polished appearance were beginning to wilt under the stress of the great effort he had made to please them. Mrs. McNamara noticed his trembling hands. She arranged to bring the dinner guests back into the living room for coffee. Then she settled the guest of honor into a comfortable chair.

A strange lull settled like a canopy over the evening. Evan Montmorency, numbed and distant, sat looking at his suit of fine clothes as if a stranger occupied them. Cousin Cleo captured Dylan Forde as her partner on the couch, but he ducked behind a wall of reserve. Neither of them spoke to Sybilla. Jenny was awed by the adult world in which she felt like a clumsy intruder. She searched for some healing topic of conversation but nothing would come. Her parents found themselves chatting awkwardly to themselves. Then Sybilla sprang to her feet.

"Once I promised to sing for you," she cried out, "and now I will keep that promise."

Dylan went with her to his apartment to fetch her guitar. When they came back he had obviously forgiven her, and they were both smiling. She seated herself as simply as a child on the floor. Mrs. McNamara turned out all the lights and brought a candle from the dinner table. Sybilla's face bloomed like a flower in its radiance. Her eyes were dark still waters. They listened to her, leaning peacefully against the strong cradle of melody.

> "*Alas, my love, you do me wrong*
> *To cast me off discourteously* . . ."

Her hands were strong and supple on the mellow instrument.

> "*And I have lovéd you so long*
> *Delighting in your company* . . .
> *Greensleeves was all my joy,*
> *Greensleeves was my delight* . . ."

The little song had bridged the wear and tear of centuries. Perhaps even Shakespeare, who had been so fond of music, had once sung it to his Dark Lady.

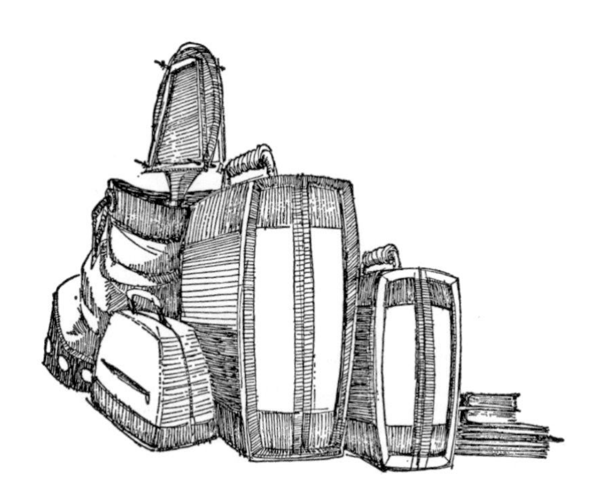

18

THERE WAS a new and pleasant development. Jenny told her parents how unhappy she was that Sarah had to leave Stratford, and after a private discussion they invited her friend to stay on with them for a few weeks. The only obstacle to the whole idea was Sarah's doting mother and father.

"I just don't know what to say. It's a lovely idea . . ." Mrs. Kaplan's deep voice quavered. "And Sarah's talked about nothing but puppets for days. Jenny is a perfectly dear child . . . but — "

Mr. Kaplan, who rarely spoke, opened his mouth. "We've never been parted from her. I don't know what we'd do without her."

"We'll take good care of her," Mrs. McNamara promised, putting her hand on Sarah's shoulder.

"I just don't know what to say," repeated Mrs. Kaplan. "She's just a baby, you know."

"Mama, I'm almost fourteen years old," Sarah said. "I haven't worn diapers for years. I can tie my own shoelaces. *Please* let me stay."

"Just think, Mrs. Kaplan," Jenny spoke up, "of how hot New York City will be. All those sweaty people . . . all those germs!"

"And remember the water shortage," Sarah said. "Before we left I could hardly brush my teeth — or take a bath! It was very unsanitary."

Her parents looked as if they both suffered from a severe stomachache.

"Please." Sarah hugged them both. "Next summer Jenny can come and stay with us."

Mrs. Kaplan made up their minds. "All right," she said courageously. "I'll pack your things."

But when they were ready to leave for home there was a tense moment when Jenny was sure they would change their decision. Sam Kaplan seemed to be glued to the handle of Sarah's suitcase. Dr. McNamara managed to pry his fingers loose and escort him to the car, but nobody could persuade him to enter it. Mrs. Kaplan's swollen eyes were hidden by her handkerchief. Cousin Cleo managed to get in everyone's way and offered so many road directions that Mr. Kaplan was finally driven into the front seat, where he slammed the door on her map. Only Sarah seemed unmoved by such abundant emotion. She kissed her parents, wished them a safe and speedy trip, and when the car had finally inched down the street under a shower of farewells she turned to Jenny with a broad smile.

"Well, that's that," she said.

On Sunday she insisted they attend the National Youth Festival concert. Jenny balked.

"Who wants to see a bunch of kids slaughter Schubert?" she asked.

"I do," Sarah said. "Maybe you'll be surprised."

Jenny was. She found the young musicians skilled beyond anything she could imagine. She thought of the thousands of dull hours they must have spent practicing for this bright moment. She recognized one of the artists — a lumpy girl from Toronto who always lugged her tuba with her on the bus.

"I used to feel sorry for her," Jenny whispered.

"Don't ever feel sorry for people who use their talent," Sarah flashed back. "Only for people who don't."

Inspired, Jenny went home to practice feverishly on the oboe while her father packed up his books and papers and hid in the bathroom. Cousin Cleo had also acquired a new roommate. It was a brave but battered French horn which the Cardiff sisters had found for her when they learned she had mastered the instrument years ago in boarding school. Now she trotted to rehearsals every morning and took her place beside Mrs. Cardiff and a safe distance from Sybilla. Although she had been persuaded to be the bassoon,

Sybilla was always late. When she did arrive she was much more eager to direct than to be directed.

"Sybilla, you must stick to being just an instrument," Olivia told her frankly. "After the puppet show you may sing for the children, but during the rest of the show you must behave and not interfere with the rest of us."

Offended, the folksinger rolled her despairing eyes. "Amateurs! How can I stand by and let you disgrace yourselves!"

Toby had erected screens so that the actor-musicians were hidden from the audience. The Cardiff sisters were skilled at manipulating the puppets, and Olivia's stage directions were crisp and confident. Only Jenny was visible as she sat on a low stool to one side.

The play date was finally fixed for a morning and an afternoon performance near the end of July. The local librarian urged the children who attended her weekly story hour to be sure to attend. Rosalind painted posters, which were pasted up in store windows. The *Beacon Herald* sent out a photographer to take a picture of the company, and they all laughed at the result. Only the puppets looked at all composed — and Sarah, who felt rather professional about publicity.

Jenny was sure it would rain. She looked for Humphrey one afternoon and found him, under a peaked baseball cap, in his basement workshop. He was bent over a strange contraption. Wires and cables sprang out in all directions. It looked like an electric octopus.

"What's that, Humphrey?" she asked.

"Can't you read?" he said. "It says PRIVATE — DO NOT ENTER on the basement door."

"I know. I forgot," she said. "Is it going to rain on Saturday?"

"No," he said.

"Are you sure?" she said. "It's important, Humphrey. If it rains our puppet show will have to be postponed."

"It won't rain," he said. "Now go away. I'm busy."

"What *is* that?"

"A secret invention."

"Will it make you famous?" she asked. Humphrey rarely smiled. Now he beamed all over.

"Yes," he said.

On Friday night there was a swift spatter of rain on the roof. Jenny gloomed all evening. Sarah practiced on her clarinet and flute, rolled up her hair in jumbo curlers, and just before bed ate a giant pizza. Later Jenny lay awake smelling pepperoni and listening resentfully to her friend's relaxed breathing. She was positive there were broken bricks under her mattress. The rush of the rain and the ticking of the clock annoyed her. Suddenly she sat straight up in bed.

"I'm scared," she said. Sarah groaned and flattened her head under the pillow. The apartment was dense with silence. Everyone had retired hours ago, and she had never felt so alone in her life. She wished she could talk to Toby and find out if he had ever experienced stagefright. She doubted if anyone had ever felt so terrified.

There was a noise downstairs, as if the front door had opened and softly closed. Footsteps seemed to move down the hall. Maybe she would be murdered in her bed. At least she would be able to stop worrying about *Peter and the Wolf*. But there was no further sound. She finally lay back and felt herself slipping into sleep.

When she awoke in the morning her mother was sitting on the edge of the bed staring at her.

"What is it?" Jenny sat up.

"Shhhhhh. Come out into the hall."

Jenny closed the bedroom door so that Sarah wouldn't be disturbed. She turned toward her mother. "Has something happened? There's something wrong, isn't there?"

"Toby called a few minutes ago," her mother told her. "The puppet show will have to be postponed."

"Why? Is it still raining?"

"No, it's a perfect day. Last night someone broke into their yard. Toby had thrown a canvas over the stage, but it was thrown aside and everything was smashed to pieces."

Quick tears warmed Jenny's eyes. Mrs. McNamara lightly touched her hair. "I'm so sorry."

"But why? Who would do such a thing?"

"I don't know."

"Oh, Mother." Jenny leaned against her. "The children will be so disappointed. And we worked so hard."

"I know. But at least the puppets are safe."

Sarah, her eyes puffy, staggered into the hall under an enormous sleep bonnet. Jenny told her what had happened.

"Well," Sarah yawned, "we'll just have to go ahead with it."

"It took Toby days to build that stage!"

"So we'll improvise . . . use a cardboard box or something. After all," she said, "the play's the thing. Even Shakespeare said so, didn't he?"

She went into the bathroom and started brushing her teeth.

"Sarah's right." Mrs. McNamara looked more cheerful. "You know, the Elizabethan players often traveled from place to place to put on their shows, and they had to adapt to all sorts of situations. They could set themselves up in a hall or an innyard and make do with whatever conditions they found. You'll have to do the same."

Sarah came out, her mouth foaming, and waved the toothbrush.

"We still have the puppets and the performers," she said. "Call Toby and see what he thinks."

Toby was miserable and furious. But he admitted that with a box and some blankets they would be able to carry on.

"Come on over," he told Jenny. "We'll go ahead with the eleven o'clock performance. But I'll need some help."

Before they arrived at the big back yard on Queen

Street they could hear the excited voices. Children hung on the fence, cluttered up the back steps, and somersaulted in the grass. They had come to see a show, and they were not going to be disappointed.

Toby and his sisters had found a packing crate and put up a wooden frame to which they attached curtains. Blankets were draped over chairs to conceal the performers. It was crude, unattractive and hasty, but it was a stage. Cousin Cleo arrived, embracing her French horn.

"Hey! That's no kid," a young spectator scornfully observed. "She's old enough to be my grandmother."

"If I were your grandmother," Miss McNamara said sharply, "I'd see to it that you soon improved your manners."

Out on the street another dramatic arrival occurred. Dark-goggled, helmeted and mysterious, Sybilla stalked through a dazzled congregation.

"Who are you?" ventured one little girl.

"I am a bassoon," Sybilla replied in her most thrilling tones. Mute with admiration, they trooped after her. Toby motioned for all the children to sit down and be quiet. Jenny sat down on the stool and tried to stop her knees from dancing.

"Look — she's shivering!" This loud voice belonged to a little boy, whose sister tried to cork him, but too late. "She's scared," he finished.

Toby came over, and rumpled Jenny's hair. "Ready?"

"No," she croaked. "I'm sick."

"You're not," he whispered, "Just frightened."

"It feels the same."

"You'll be fine. Just remember that everything depends on you."

"*Thanks,* Toby. Now I feel worse."

"Ladies and gentlemen . . ." The children sent up a whoop of excitement. "We take great pleasure in presenting . . ." Jenny met and answered Toby's wide smile. "*Peter and the Wolf.*"

19

THERE had never been a more appreciative audience. That was decided in the evening as the two families met to celebrate the success of the puppet show. The children had giggled and gasped, chuckled and cheered. As they ate a picnic supper on the island, all the talk revolved around *Peter and the Wolf*. Cousin Cleo, her flaming face cooled by a large straw hat, had brought Evan Montmorency. Sybilla was with Dylan Forde.

"Someone asked for my autograph," Jenny glowed.

"You were very good," Alexander Cardiff told her. "Not just good — but very good."

The words wove a pleasant melody inside her head. She repeated them to herself.

"The best part is being asked to do the show again," said Rosalind. Her deep dimples flashed. "The Lions Club would like us to put it on for some handicapped children."

"And they want to pay us," chirped Olivia. "It's too good to be true."

"That will make us professionals," said beautiful Mrs. Cardiff.

"I already am a professional," Sybilla reminded them huskily.

"The children loved it when you asked them to join in the singing," Viola said generously, blowing up her hair. "It made them feel a part of it, Sybilla."

Portia's only remark came from inside a hamburger roll. "Pickles," she demanded, "please."

Sybilla busied herself with Dylan's plate.

"Don't cut my chicken for me," he complained. "I can do it myself."

"Eat your salad, Dylan." Wildly she agitated her elbows, scattering flies and knocking over the iced tea. "You need vitamins, vitamins, vitamins."

"I don't like vegetables."

"Silly." She picked up a carrot stick and pushed it between his lips. "Be a good little bunny, darling. Eat your carrot."

He did as he was told. The day, which had been harsh with sun, now softened into early evening. A breeze moved lightly among them. Jenny was full of happiness. She left the table. Down by the Avon she knelt and dipped her hands into the cool water.

Toby had been very quiet during the meal. Now as the adults lingered over coffee he strolled over and joined her.

"What is it, Toby?"

"It's my mother. I'm awfully worried about her."

"You've had another phone call?"

"Yes. They stopped for a while after we got an unlisted number. Now they've started again. She isn't sleeping very well."

"I'm so sorry, Toby. I wish there were something I could do."

"If I ever find out — " his voice broke.

"I remember the first day I met you, and how frightened your sister was then. Will you tell me what that was all about?"

"We'd had another phone call," he admitted. "That time someone whispered that Dad had been in a terrible accident. Then we found out that it was another hoax."

Talking quietly, they drifted around the perimeter of the island. They heard Sybilla's shouts of laughter and Evan Montmorency's voice as he recited snatches of poetry.

"I'm glad Cousin Cleo brought him tonight," Jenny said. "She's taken him under her wing. You don't still think he has anything to do with these calls, do you?"

Toby looked uncomfortable. "I don't want to suspect anyone, Jenny," he said, "and I'm sure he would never have wrecked our stage. But I think he may have a grudge against Dad, and you told me yourself that he was close to Exhibition Hall the day that exhibit was ruined."

"You're wrong!" Her voice rang out. "I just know you're wrong."

Several people walking nearby looked at her curiously.

"You needn't be angry," he said. "I hope I am."

Abruptly Jenny turned and moved quickly back toward the picnickers. Her mother was cleaning up the table.

"It's getting late, honey," she said. "Toby and Dylan and Mr. Cardiff have to get over to the Festival Theatre, and we don't want to be late for *Don Giovanni.*"

Slowly the families broke apart and scattered their goodnights on the evening air. Sybilla led Dylan away by the wrist, and his plaintive protests floated back to them.

"You treat me like a child, Sybilla."

"But you are a child."

"Poor Dylan," Sarah sighed. "I feel so sorry for him when Sybilla bullies him."

"There's someone else I feel sorry for," Jenny whispered, as they approached their apartment house. Humphrey, a shapeless lump, sat rocking on the porch. "It's as if he's deaf and blind to the whole world."

"Once I moved a stone," Sarah said as they climbed

the stairs, "and found a toad. I'll never forget how I felt. It's the same when I see Humphrey."

The downtown theatre, the Avon, had once been a home for touring plays and musical comedies. After that it had served as the local movie house. When the Stratford Festival became a successful enterprise the old Avon had been purchased and redecorated. Here the more modern plays, the ballet and the opera were performed. Here the McNamaras had already seen the controversial new play *Speak Muse*. All the actors wore hammered metal masks and spoke in hollow mournful voices.

"It's very avant-garde," her father had told her.

"What does that mean?"

"Modern. Ahead of the times."

"You mean that someday I will understand what it was all about?"

"Yes, probably."

"Then I hope I live that long," Jenny said. "I'd really like to know what I missed."

Tonight was the performance of the opera that Sarah had been so anxious to see. In the lobby Jenny's parents bumped into some old friends, and the two girls stood apart to watch the people crowd inside.

"There's the playwright who wrote *Speak Muse,*" Sarah whispered. "I've seen his picture in the New York *Times*."

They stared. A handsome young man in a checked waistcoat stood in the middle of an attentive group.

Talking rapidly, he took a coin purse out of his pocket, opened it, and swiftly brought his fingers up to his face.

"What's he doing?" Jenny was horrified. "Putting money up his nose?"

"I don't know," Sarah said. "Maybe it's nasal spray."

The young playwright uttered a shattering sneeze. The group around him heaved with admiration, and then the conversation raced away once again. Sarah chuckled.

"He's taking snuff."

"I thought only dirty old men did that."

"No, he's an intellectual."

"How can you tell?"

"Because you can't understand a word he's saying."

"Don't intellectuals ever make sense?"

"Hardly ever," Sarah said with a grin, "except at dinner. Then they say 'pass the butter, please' just like everybody else."

They went inside and took their seats. Jenny admired the golden brocaded walls and the starry splash of light which radiated from an overhead chandelier.

"*Don Giovanni* is one of the greatest operas of all time," Sarah said. She was often as determined to be instructive as Cousin Cleo. "Some people think it's Mozart's best."

"All I know about opera," Jenny noted, "is that when anyone gets murdered everyone stands around and sings."

"If they stood around and talked," Sarah said, "it would be a play. Or if they stood around and danced, it would be a ballet."

"I don't know why they stand around at all," Jenny concluded. "If I saw a murder I'd *run*."

"But that wouldn't be art." Sarah flipped her long hair over her shoulders and consulted her program notes. "You're in luck," she told Jenny. "This performance is in English translation."

Dr. and Mrs. McNamara took their seats, and Cousin Cleo, in a rustle of dark silk, roosted next to Jenny. She took out a tiny pair of binoculars and scanned the audience.

"Why did you bring those?" Jenny whispered.

"These are my opera glasses. It's a custom, Jenny."

The overture began. Jenny wondered if it was also the custom when the gentleman behind her began to hum along with the orchestra. His peppermint breath scorched the back of her neck. The musical prologue, like a knife on flint, sharpened the appetite for the feast to come.

The curtain had barely gone up before the rascally Don Giovanni murdered the father of Donna Anna and burst into glorious song. "See what I mean?" Jenny poked Sarah.

Donna Anna, a towering rectangle of rage, mourned her father's death while her fiancé vowed vengeance on the murderer.

"I think she's hefty enough to take care of her own

vengeance," Jenny whispered. "She's bigger than he is."

"She may look like a halfback," said Sarah primly, as the music and action rushed along, "but she sings like an angel." Donna Elvira, the lovely young woman once jilted by Don Giovanni, tossed out a beautiful aria. A sparkling peasant girl, Zerlina, appeared and danced about the stage.

"She'll fall in love with him too," Sarah warned.

"I thought she was supposed to marry Masetto." Jenny tried to read the program notes in the dark.

"Wait and see!"

There was an exciting scene where Don Giovanni was confronted by his masked pursuers and then escaped. The first act was over, and Jenny realized she was having a wonderful time.

During intermission her father excused himself to talk with a broad man in a lavender shirt. She asked her mother who he was.

"That's Lister LeRoy. He's a famous theatre critic from Toronto."

"Why does he look so angry? Isn't he enjoying himself?"

"He didn't come to enjoy himself," Maggie McNamara said sensibly. "He came to criticize the performance."

"You mean that's his job? He gets paid for it?"

"Of course."

"Cousin Cleo criticizes everything — for nothing."

Her mother laughed. "But she's not a professional."

"Why must people be told what's good or bad about a show? Don't they know whether or not they like it?"

"Some people like to be told if they *should*."

Jenny shook her head. "I don't need Lister LeRoy to tell me I should like *Don Giovanni*," she said. "Life must be very complicated when you grow up."

Her mother squeezed her hand. "It is, sometimes."

During the second half of the opera there was a scene in the churchyard. Arrogantly Don Giovanni invited the stone statue of the man he had murdered, the Commendatore, to come and dine with him that evening. Jenny felt suddenly protective toward Don Giovanni. She wished he would repent of all his bad deeds. She watched him gnaw on a chicken bone and wash it down on a wave of wine.

Cousin Cleo was mesmerized. "Appalling table manners," she shuddered, "but he certainly has style."

Then came the thrilling conclusion when the massive stone statue of the Commendatore appeared before Don Giovanni, who refused to repent and was dragged, kicking and screaming, down to Hell. Loud applause recalled the sinner from fire and brimstone to take his curtain calls. Then it was over, and the audience began to leave the theatre. Jenny, still brimming with music and passion, felt that if she moved she would spill over like a tipped jug.

20

SUMMER turned a corner into August, and cars still streamed endlessly into the city. People flowed continuously through the streets. Every country and every tongue was represented, but the common language was Shakespeare, and the air hummed with talk. Longhaired students stood on street corners to discuss hotly the performance they had just seen; husbands and wives argued in restaurants over the merits of one actor against another; broad-bottomed matrons on bicycles went by lilting Mozartian airs. Scholars blundered through stoplights reading poetry while families drifted on the river, chanting blank verse.

"New York is alive like this," Sarah observed one

morning at breakfast. "People there seem to be caught up in something larger and more exciting than the details of their own little lives."

Maggie McNamara set a stack of pancakes down in front of each girl and passed the syrup.

"Where is Cousin Cleo?" Jenny asked.

"She's already gone to see Evan Montmorency. They've been working on his memoirs every morning, you know. She's very optimistic."

"Poor man. She'll talk him to death."

"I don't think so. She's helped, I think, by being so interested in him. He seems more in touch with reality — much less eccentric."

"How did you like *King Lear?*" Sarah asked. She had already seen the play with her parents, and had been asleep when the McNamaras arrived home the night before.

"I'll be honest," said Jenny, mopping butter off her chin. "I know it was a brilliant performance, and that Miss Fitzsimmons is a great Cordelia and that Lister LeRoy would say I ought to like it. But I didn't. It was just too sad. I kept wishing that King Lear would hiccup. I needed to laugh, and instead I sat there and cried."

Sarah scoffed, "Jenny, you're so immature."

"I know. I guess I'm just not ready for tragedy."

"Will you come with me to the Rothman Galleries?" her friend asked. "They have an exhibit of that famous Canadian painter — Thomson. Tom Thomson."

Jenny vigorously indicated she would not. "No, I already feel just like a sausage. I'm so crammed with culture that if you stuck a fork in me I'd burst."

"You haven't seen much of Toby lately, have you?" said her mother.

"No. That's where I'm going today."

It was after lunch when she arrived at the big house on Queen Street. The back door was half open, but nobody answered her knock. She stepped into the kitchen. Fat Falstaff was huddled mournfully over his dish. When he saw her he gave a pitiful sigh and licked the empty saucer. Pistol leaped from a chair, gave a scream of rage, and tore off down the hall. Jenny realized that the cats hadn't been fed.

Something was wrong. The house was too quiet. The table was set, and there was a pot of cold soup on the stove. Overhead she heard Pistol utter a sudden horrible yowl. It sounded as if someone had stepped on his tail. She tiptoed to the bottom of the stairs.

"Is anybody home?" Her voice quivered. "Is anybody up there?"

She could hear the orchestration of a dozen busy clocks.

"Pistol?"

The house exploded into sound. It was one o'clock, and there was a wild bonging and clanging and chirping from every part of the house. The hamster in the kitchen woke up and began a frantic race on his exercise wheel. Jenny fled.

Something had happened in the apartment on Elizabeth Street. Her parents sat solemnly in the living room talking in low voices as she came in. They didn't seem aware that the teakettle shrieked on the kitchen range. Jenny turned it off, and then went in to see them. Her father smoked a pipe he had forgotten to light.

"We'd like to talk to you, Jenny."

"Yes?"

"We're going to send Sarah home."

"Daddy!"

"You and your mother will be leaving Stratford by the end of the week."

"But why? What's happened?"

He handed her a copy of the *Beacon Herald*. She read the headline on the front page: THEATRE THREATENED.

"What's this all about?"

"Someone has actually threatened to blow up the Festival Theatre," her mother said. New, sharp creases had formed on each side of her mouth.

"That's ridiculous. It's a joke."

"I don't think so," Dr. McNamara said. "Too many peculiar things have happened. I won't risk keeping you here, and I'm responsible for Sarah too."

"I won't go!"

"Oh, Jenny." Her father drew her close to him. "It wasn't very long ago that you said you wouldn't come."

"We can't go. We haven't seen all the plays. The ballet opens next week."

"It's decided." Maggie McNamara spoke firmly. "Your father will stay on and finish his research, and I expect Cousin Cleo will probably want to stay with him."

"I don't like to think what this threat will do to the Festival," the professor said. "I imagine a lot of people will be frightened away."

The telephone rang.

"I have to see you, Jenny." It was Toby. She hadn't heard from him since the evening they had quarreled.

"I was just over at your house, Toby."

"Were the cats here then?"

"Yes, why?"

"They've both disappeared."

"Toby!"

"Could you meet me after the matinee — at the Shakespearean Gardens?"

"Yes."

"I'll see you then."

When she reached the park late in the afternoon Toby was already there. Through the stout wooden arches which supported the thatched roof of the entrance she saw sunlight ripple like bright water on the hedges. Her footsteps crunched over the gravel.

"Have you found your cats yet?"

"No." He explained: "We got a call this morning. It said the police wanted to see us all down at the station. Of course they hadn't really called us at all. When we got home the cats were missing."

"But I was there! Someone may have been right in the house then!"

Discouraged, Toby picked up a handful of stones and began to pitch them angrily over a hedge. "I don't know how much more my mother can take," he said. "Will you help me find out who is doing these things to us, Jenny?"

"I wish I could." She broke the news that she had to leave Stratford at the end of the week.

"Because of this bomb threat? I don't blame your father. Now I know that Evan Montmorency isn't involved. He simply isn't capable of this kind of malice."

"Haven't you any other ideas, Toby?"

"I thought of someone today . . . a yardman Dad hired last summer. We had to let him go because he never seemed to do anything right. He seemed pretty harmless at the time, but now I wonder."

"What was his name?"

"I don't even remember. It always reminded me of Humpty Dumpty."

"It wasn't Humphrey Dumphrie, was it?"

"Yes, that's it! Do you know him?"

"He's our landlord. But he never mentioned working for you before," Jenny said. "He always refers to you as 'that crazy family on Queen Street.' "

Toby managed a smile. "That doesn't mean anything. A lot of people might think that."

Jenny thought of something else. "He could have seen your unlisted telephone number, too. I have it written down right beside the telephone in the kitchen."

"Will you keep an eye on him, Jenny? There isn't much time left."

They walked home together. Stratford was noticeably tense. Everywhere people stood and talked about the shocking item in the newspaper. Speeding madly, Sybilla roared by on her motorcycle and waved at them. A traffic policeman in his patrol car raced after her.

Jenny was glad to have something to laugh about.

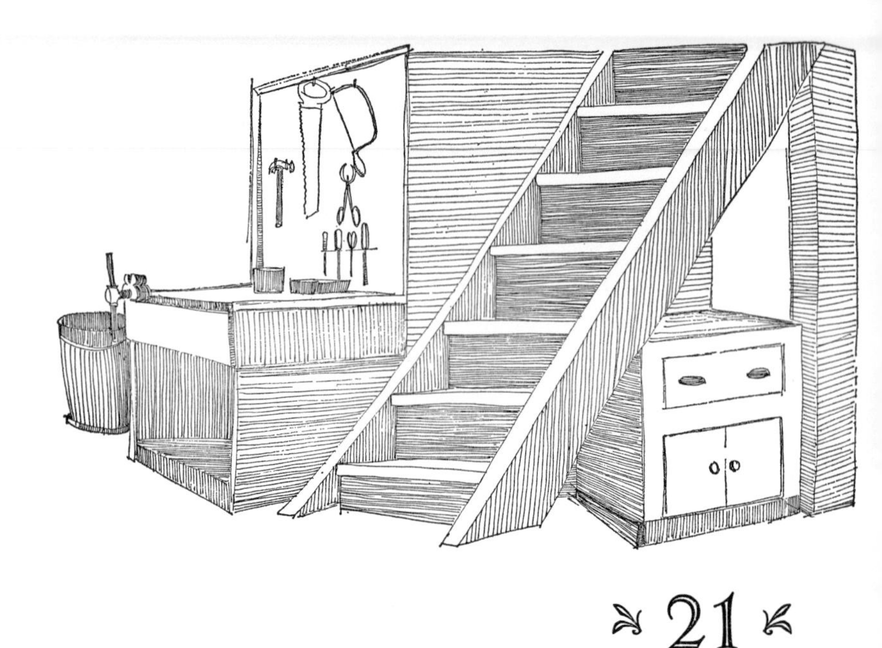

21

DINNER was dreary. Rain rapped softly against the windows, and there was an occasional thud of thunder that sounded like someone falling out of bed. Nobody had anything to say — except Cousin Cleo. Challenged by all the empty silence, she felt compelled to fill it up.

"Mad bombers are a disgrace," she observed.

Sarah sniffed. Her face, blotchy from crying, looked like the mottled map of a foreign country.

Cousin Cleo tried again. "Miss Fitzsimmons is in love with a jockey," she said.

Sarah pinched off another sniff with her handkerchief, and Dr. McNamara looked provoked.

"Miss Fitzsimmons is already married," he said sternly, "to an exceedingly tall Irish politician. Please stop babbling, Cleo."

"This pot roast is scorched!" she retorted, hurling down her napkin. "I'm going to go and read the *National Geographic.*"

"She's upset," Mrs. McNamara whispered. "Be nice to her this evening. Daddy and I have to go out for a little while."

After they left the apartment the girls went into the living room.

"Would you like to watch television with us?" Jenny suggested.

"It warps the mind," her cousin warned. "All that bloodshed and violence."

"Shakespeare's plays are full of bloodshed and violence, too," Sarah said.

"It's a question of taste," Cousin Cleo replied loftily. "Shakespeare's characters die poetically . . . like beautiful, broken birds." She stared, openmouthed, as a cowboy gunned down four of his best friends and moseyed off into the sunset. "How dreadful!"

"I'll change the channel." Jenny reached for the dial, but her cousin caught her wrist.

"You girls run along and do the dishes. I'll change it myself."

In the kitchen Jenny ran hot water into the sink and thoughtfully stirred the soapsuds.

"I'm going down there."

"Down where?"

"To Humphrey's workshop in the basement."

"But he's not there," Sarah told her, reaching for a dish towel. "He always takes his mother to the supermarket on Thursday nights."

"I know. That's why I'm going down now."

"What's the matter with you, Jenny?"

Jenny looked peculiar. "I think I'm having an attack," she said.

Sarah backed into the refrigerator. "Attack of what?" she asked suspiciously.

"It's nothing contagious." Jenny planted plates in the rubber rack. "It's just that my imagination gets overheated sometimes, like a radiator. That's when I'm sure I have a rare and fatal disease, or when I think I hear burglars in the closet. An overheated imagination can be a very dangerous thing."

Sarah was wary. "I guess so," she said.

"That's why I've learned never to trust myself when I'm having an attack," Jenny went on. "So maybe that thing down there isn't a bomb after all."

Sarah dropped knives and forks all over the kitchen floor. Her face faded to the waxy color of a candle.

"What thing . . . where?"

"That contraption Humphrey has been working on. I saw it once when I went down to ask about the weather."

"And you think it could be a bomb?"

"I just think I ought to have another look."

"Your cousin won't let you."

"I think she's busy warping her mind right now," Jenny said, opening the kitchen door a crack. There was a rattle of gunfire and the sounds of a lively stampede thundering through the living room. "You can help me."

"You want *me* to go down there?"

"No. Just keep watch in case they come back too soon."

Cautiously Jenny slipped into the hall and tiptoed down the creaky stairs. When she reached the basement door she ignored the sign: PRIVATE — DO NOT ENTER. She turned the knob and inched down into a damp and twilight place, careful to look for spiders. Everything seemed as neat and innocent as a nursery. Humphrey's tools hung from a pegboard. The shelves were lined with garden supplies, paint cans, and shiny jars of preserves. There was no sign of the electric octopus. Jenny rummaged through a stack of *Popular Mechanics* and then pulled open the heavy drawer of the workbench. Inside was a scrapbook. She took it out and opened the cover.

"Jenny!" Sarah's face was a white blob at the top of the stairs. "I think they're coming back. I heard the car."

Jenny took another quick glance at the clippings in the scrapbook. Then she shoved it back and tried to shut the drawer. It had jammed. She wrenched the drawer free and slammed it tightly, then scrambled for the stairs.

It was too late. Humphrey's boots were on the top step. His body loomed grotesquely above, and behind him shifted the nervous shadow of his mother.

"You'd better come up," he said, in his flat heavy way, "and tell us what you're doing down there."

"Oh, hello, Humphrey . . . Mrs. Dumphrie." Jenny found it hard to hold the smile which wobbled on her face. "I thought you had gone shopping or I'd have asked you first."

Rain dripped from Humphrey's peaked baseball cap. His cheeks, angry and putty-colored, glistened with moisture.

"Asked me about what?"

"Well, I told you before that the electric cord on our toaster was getting pretty frayed. Now it's useless. I came down to get another."

Slowly she climbed the stairs to meet them face to face.

"Nobody is allowed in my workshop," he growled.

"Goodness." Her laugh shook. "You know I wouldn't touch anything I wasn't supposed to. But we really could use that cord."

"He'll get one for you first thing in the morning," Mrs. Dumphrie promised.

"Thanks a lot. Goodnight!" She hopped up to the second-story landing two steps at a time. Sarah grabbed her at the top.

"Did he catch you?"

"Yes. I told him we needed an electric cord — and we do."

Back in the apartment they could hear the TV marshal say he'd never yet shot a man without being sorry for it.

"Did you find anything?" Sarah asked.

"Not what I was looking for," Jenny admitted. "But something almost as frightening. Humphrey keeps a scrapbook about bombings — parliament buildings, airplane terminals, bus depots. I think he *may* be planning to blow up the Festival Theatre. But how can we be sure?"

"It reminds me of *Hamlet,*" Sarah said. "Have you seen it?"

"No."

Sarah explained. "Hamlet was the Prince of Denmark, see? And his father was murdered. Then Hamlet's uncle married the widowed queen right away and became king."

Jenny was impatient. "What does that have to do with Humphrey?"

Sarah disappeared into the dining room. When she came back she was a tall shape, shrouded under a tablecloth. Her voice was muffled.

"The ghost of Hamlet's father came back and told him what had happened." She walked stiffly around the kitchen like a sleepwalker, with her hands raised in front.

The tension broke. Jenny laughed. "What did Hamlet do then?"

"Nothing. He decided to trap the king into revealing his guilt."

"How did he manage that?"

Sarah popped out from under the cloth. She began to caper around the kitchen, and stubbed her toe on the wastebasket.

"A group of traveling players arrived at the castle. Hamlet made up his own play and asked them to put it on. The players acted out the murder of his father just the way it happened — by pouring poison in his ear."

"In his ear!"

"Anyway," Sarah continued, "the king was so upset that he stood up and screamed, 'Give me some light.' And he sent the players away."

Jenny was mystified. "This is all very interesting," she said, "but how does it help us?"

"We could do the same thing," Sarah said. "Invite Humphrey to a puppet show, and then point the finger of suspicion at him."

"It won't work." Jenny was positive. "In the first place he wouldn't come. In the second place he might not be guilty of anything. And in the third — he'd never scream for light. He just doesn't have the imagination."

"Then what will we do?"

"Call Toby in the morning and tell him what we've discovered."

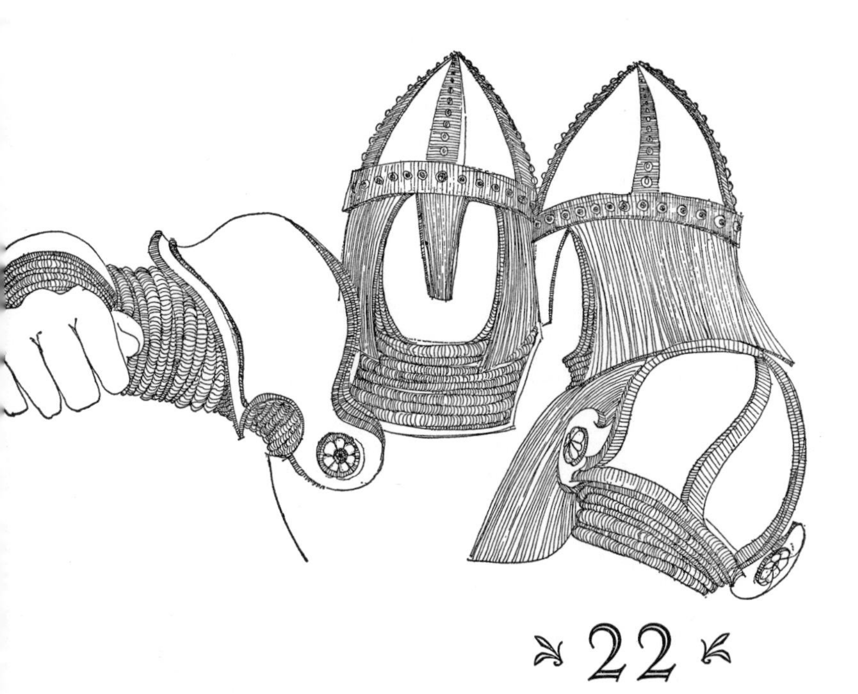

22

"JENNY."

Dr. McNamara stood in the doorway. "Mr. Cardiff is here. He'd like to talk to you."

Jenny leaped off the bed, where she and Sarah had been playing a mournful duet with clarinet and oboe. The actor's strong face looked old and tired above his crisp shirt collar.

"Have you seen Toby today?" he asked immediately.

"No, Mr. Cardiff. I did talk to him on the telephone this morning."

"Did he say where he was going?"

"No."

His laugh sounded forced. "Well, he'll turn up. He didn't come home for lunch, and of course his mother is very worried."

"Sarah and I will look for him," Jenny volunteered.

"Would you? Toby's never been irresponsible. I guess I'm a little worried too, Jenny."

"We'll go right away," she promised.

In the hall she and Sarah ran into Dylan Forde.

"You haven't seen Toby Cardiff, have you?" Jenny asked him.

"No." He looked worried and preoccupied too.

"Mr. Forde," she asked, "do you think someone is going to try to blow up the theatre?"

"We're concerned," he said, and then managed one of his tiny smiles. "It's a little like hearing the astonishing news that someone wants to do away with your mother. You feel frightened — and outraged — and curiously helpless. I never fully realized just how important the Festival Theatre was to me until it was threatened. Now I'm angry — deeply angry."

"Are the performances going on as scheduled?"

"Of course. But to much smaller houses. Every safety precaution has been taken."

"What does Sybilla think of all this?"

"Sybilla," he said, "seldom, if ever, thinks at all. She'd like me to stay home and hide my head under the covers until it all blows over. Sybilla," he concluded, "is a child."

He waved and went down the hall. For the next couple of hours Jenny and Sarah wove back and forth across the city searching for Toby. They covered the island and the tennis courts and the Shakespearean Gardens, but there was no sign of him.

"I feel responsible," Jenny told her friend. "I did tell him about that scrapbook this morning. He did get excited about it. I hope he hasn't done anything foolish."

"Maybe he's already at home," Sarah said. "After all, he has a performance tonight. I think we'd better go back to your place."

They met Cousin Cleo on her way out of the apartment.

"Evan has asked me to have dinner with him," she told them. "Your parents will be home any minute, Jenny. By the way, your friend Toby called. He left a number and asked if you'd get in touch with him right away."

Relieved, Jenny opened the door. Sarah's eyes were round as dimes.

"Did you see that dress your cousin was wearing?" she asked. "It was pink — with ruffles!"

"Did you see her shoes? They had high heels!"

Sarah was concerned. "I hope she makes it down . . ."

There was a distant crash. Miss McNamara, in stocking feet, wobbled back up the stairs. She went into her bedroom, rummaged under her dresser, and came out wearing her old walking shoes. From the knees up she was still coquette, but from the knees down she was comfortable.

"Handsome is as handsome does," she said, and went out slamming the door.

Jenny quickly dialed the number on the telephone pad.

"Where are you?" she asked as soon as she heard Toby's voice.

"At the theatre."

"Does your father know? He's worried about you."

"Yes. I just called home. I told him I'd see him tonight at *Henry the Fifth*."

"Where have you been, Toby?"

"I can't talk now. I only called to ask a favor. It's terribly important."

"What is it?"

"I may not make that performance tonight. I want you to take my place."

"I can't!"

"Yes, you can. We're the same size. You'll only be on for a few scenes, and you'll be wearing a helmet. Nicky will help. In fact, he's waiting here for you right now."

"I won't do it."

"Don't tell anyone, Jenny. You promised you'd help."

She hesitated a fraction of a second too long.

"Thanks," he said, and hung up.

Two hours later Jenny found herself skulking around corners backstage at the great theatre inside a suit of armor. Nicky had waited while she wriggled into the costume behind a sofa in the deserted lounge, and now he kept a sharp eye on her.

"You look fine," he murmured. "But quit fussing with that sword. You're acting just like a girl."

Miss Fitzsimmons, her broad Irish face wrinkled in concentration, swooshed past in a cloud of perfume and gave Jenny an affectionate pinch. She had mistaken her for Toby.

"She's saying her prayers," Nicky whispered.

"Then I'd better say mine," Jenny said. "I feel like I'm hiding in a closet. It's hot under this helmet."

"All you have to do the first time we're onstage is to follow me up the ladder."

"I'll trip."

"No you won't. Toward the end we come back and bring on the cannon."

"It's a good thing I don't have to say anything," she muttered.

"I think you've said enough already," he told her. They stood in the corridor and looked up at a row of glittering shields. He pointed. "That one's yours. And cheer up. Wait until you take that first curtain call."

Miss Timchuk passed between and shoved a bag of candy at them.

"Gumdrops, fellows?"

"No, thanks," Nicky said. "Is anybody out there, Charley?"

Her laugh was nervous. "A few. My friend Mr. Smallwood is in the front row. He says his secret information proved to be a forgery, but someday he'll prove Shakespeare was a fraud. In the meantime nothing will keep him away."

Jenny felt as if she stood in the middle of a nightmare. The other actors seemed unreal to her, dressed from another time — like magnificent ghosts out of the past who had come to strut their hour upon the stage and then to vanish. She remembered Evan Montmorency and thought of the people sitting out front who would witness her public disgrace. She wondered what on earth Sarah had told her parents. No matter how she looked at it she was in deep trouble.

A voice from behind startled her.

"Toby! I've been looking for you."

"Oh, oh," Nicky said under his breath. "It's Mr. Cardiff."

"Wait a minute, Alex. Over here, please." Max, the director, spoke up. Jenny and Nicky quickly moved out of sight.

"I can't do it," Jenny said. "If I go out there the French will probably win the Battle of Agincourt. I'll change the whole course of English history."

He only laughed. "Come on, it's time. Let's go!"

23

"YOU'RE practically a pro!" Nicky and Jenny stood in the dim tunnel underneath the auditorium and waited for their next entrance. The play was well underway, moving smoothly toward the powerful climax. Jenny leaned down to take a closer look at the small wooden cannon. She peered into the long dark barrel of the gun. "It won't really go off, will it, Nicky?"

"It couldn't hurt a flea," he reassured her. "It isn't loaded."

"But it looks loaded." She moved closer to him. More costumed figures moved up quietly to stand behind her. A spear brushed against her back and she jumped. "What's inside it?"

"Nothing at all. Now, Jenny — let's go."

"This is heavy, isn't it?" Jenny panted. Together they pushed, and the cannon rumbled up the ramp and onto the darkened stage. Quick shapes moved noiselessly around them, and she could hear the rustle of the audience only inches away. Then the lights came up. A group of English nobles discussed their chances against the overwhelming number of the French. She recognized Dylan Forde behind fierce white whiskers as Gloucester. His voice cut the air sharply:

"*Where is the King?*"

Bedford replied: "*The King himself is rode to view the battle.*"

Jenny leaned against the cannon with Nicky crouched at her heels. She could hear her heart slam against the fiberglass shell of armor. An awful suspicion had taken hold of her imagination and set it blazing ever since she looked down the gaping mouth of the gun.

Westmoreland, standing nearby, pounded his big fist on the muzzle. "*Of fighting men they have full three-score thousand,*" he shouted.

Jenny, through clenched teeth, appealed to him: "Don't do that!"

The nobles exchanged a startled glance.

"Be quiet." Nicky's voice was rigid with anger.

Jenny inched forward. His hand reached out and

gripped her ankle so hard she could feel a bruise blossom.

"Keep still," he hissed.

Stubbornly she wrenched her leg away and brought her body up a few more inches. She felt her boot come off in his hand. There was a nervous titter from the front row. She remembered the big hole in her sock, and perspiration began to drip down from under the helmet. Now she was close enough to see. Poking her head sideways, she looked once again down the long throat of the weapon. Tucked inside was just what she expected to be there. It was the electric octopus she had seen once before. Now she knew it really was a bomb.

Salisbury spoke.

> "*God bye you, Princes all; I'll to my charge.*
> *If we no more meet till we meet in heaven*"

"That's where it's going to be, all right," Jenny whispered, reaching out to yank desperately at the hem of Dylan's cloak, "unless we get this thing out of here."

"*Then joyfully, my noble Lord of Bedford,*
My dear Lord Gloucester, and my good Lord Exeter,
And my kind kinsman — warriors all, adieu!"

Surprised and distracted by Jenny's clutching fingers, Dylan forgot to shake Salisbury's extended hand. Bedford, to cover this oversight, rushed up to take it just as the confused Salisbury dropped his arm. Awkwardly Salisbury made his exit.

Now the King was onstage, standing only a few feet away. Jenny saw the bright glint of his sword. Quickly she scrambled to her feet and leaned her whole weight against the cannon. Nicky grabbed the rear wheel and held on for dear life.

"Idiot," he groaned. "Not now!"

Once more she made an appeal for help. "Dylan, it's me — Jenny! Help me get this cannon off."

There was a terrible silence. The handsome King opened his mouth to speak — and forgot his lines. Nervous laughter boiled over from somewhere in the audience. The harder Jenny tried to move the cannon the more stubbornly Nicky held it fast.

Dylan came to life. The spectacle of two foot soldiers quarreling over a silly cannon was an unexpected and embarrassing piece of slapstick. He made up his own speech, gesturing for help from his fellow actors.

"*Let's add our seasoned strength*
To this diminished store."

Jenny and Nicky panted and pulled in opposite directions.

"*These are but babes — and like spring lambs*
Ill-placéd on the field of war."

Bedford and Exeter rushed to the rescue. They added their weight to Jenny's, and the cannon shot back down the ramp. Nicky lost his grip and somersaulted upside down on the stage. Jenny did not look back. At last they were out of sight, and people were popping up from everywhere. The cannon was seized, and a group of worried-looking men bent over it like grave surgeons in an operating room. Everyone else was pushed back out of the way. Max, the director, pulling out his hair like rough grass, catapulted in five directions at the same time. Policemen poked everywhere, making little notations in their notebooks. Someone roughly took hold of Jenny's arm and hauled her away through the vast bubbling confusion as theatre officials tried to shutter up the noise and direct all the excited people back toward the Green Room.

"Would you please tell me what you were trying to do out there?" Alex Cardiff said angrily. He set her free in front of the dressing room. Jenny felt too tired to move or speak. Slowly she pulled off her helmet, and faced him.

"Jenny!" he exclaimed. "Jenny McNamara!"

"Alex — you're on in a few minutes." Max leaped out at Mr. Cardiff and hurried him away. Onstage the Battle of Agincourt boomed to a triumph, and Jenny had almost but not quite changed the course of English history. Soon King Henry the Fifth, in embossed jacket and silk tights, would lightly claim Katherine of France as his bride. The wildly excited director still tried to control the backstage traffic.

"Shhhhhhh" rippled through the crowd, and then "shhhhhhh" again, like a giant wind, but no one would be still. Jenny saw Martha Cardiff leaning against

Charlene Timchuk, and her own mother appeared, holding Sarah by the arm as if she were afraid the girl would sail off like a balloon in a gale. Then the play was over. Gusts of applause sounded like distant friendly thunder as the players combined to present themselves for the curtain call.

Nicky was at her elbow, sweat running into his eyes.

"Come on, Jenny." He guided her toward the stage.

"I won't go out there."

"You can't miss your first curtain call."

"Aren't you mad at me? Is the bomb going to explode?"

"No, it's all right. Come on."

They ran out into the lights, and after them in increasing order of importance came the principals. The applause grew with each entrance, and the rhythm of all those beating hands acknowledged a profound pleasure. As she looked into the galaxy of tiny faces Jenny decided she could spend the rest of her life happily rooted to the spot.

"You'll be back one day," Nicky assured her. "With both boots on next time."

Only then did she discover she was still wearing the sock with the hole in it.

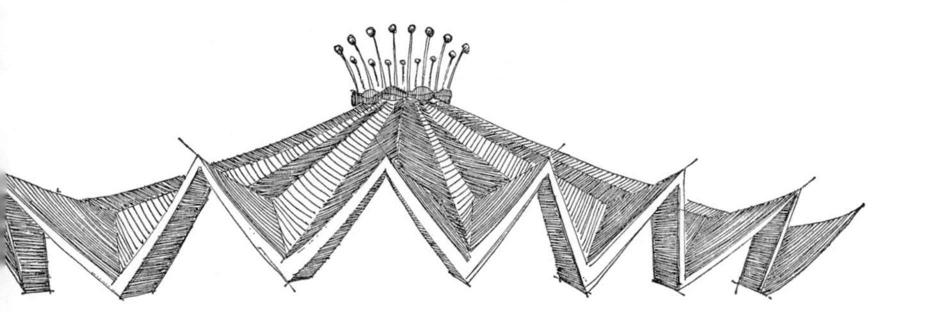

24

TOBY waited, his eyes like sparks. He danced her up and down and threw an arm around her shoulder.

"Thanks, Jenny! Are you all right?"

"Just confused," she said. "Was it Humphrey?"

"Yes. They have him outside."

"When was that bomb supposed to explode?"

"In the middle of the night, I guess. Actually it couldn't have blown up a paper bag."

"Could we go outside and get some air?"

More people surrounded the theater. Some streamed away into the night while others collected in little groups to stare at the police car parked near the curb.

Jenny saw Mrs. Cardiff walk over to it and bend down to look through a window. A policeman inside rolled down the glass.

"You won't be bothered again, Mrs. Cardiff," he said. Humphrey sat huddled in the back seat, with his close-cropped head tipped forward on his chest and his eyes downcast. Jenny, pricked by pity, thought he looked like a fat sad baby.

"What did we ever do to you, Humphrey," Mrs. Cardiff asked him quietly, "to make you hate us so?"

Humphrey moistened his lips, and struggled to form his thoughts. Finally he shrugged.

"It wasn't you," he said in a petulant voice. "You were just part of that." He pointed. Jenny looked over her shoulder at the building which looked like a king's crown all jeweled with lights. "That's what I hated. They wouldn't let me be part of it too," he said. "I didn't want to hurt anybody."

Toby took his mother's arm.

"Come on," he said. "I'm going to take you home."

"Would someone help me out of this, please?" Jenny gasped, thumping her armor. While Toby unfastened it she looked around for her parents. A plump, pimpled man rushed up and waved a pencil in her face. He wanted to know if she had discovered the bomb inside the cannon.

"Well, I did —"

"Did you know this Dumphrie put it there?"

"I wasn't sure —"

"Leave her alone." Maggie McNamara appeared

again. She still held Sarah by the arm, and her voice was cracked with strain. "She's been through enough." Dr. McNamara's car pulled up, and they shoved their way toward it through curious faces. Once inside Jenny clung to her father for a brief moment.

"Don't scold me," she asked. "Not just yet."

They drove toward Queen Street where she saw flashbulbs light the night like distant fireflies. The Cardiff house was surrounded by more strangers and reporters, and one familiar face. It was the little neighborhood boy who had to be censored by his sister. As a helpful police officer escorted Jenny toward the house he seized her with a sympathetic hand.

"What did they get you for, Jenny?" Then arms closed around her, and a deep thrilling voice momentarily stilled all the noise. She was hustled inside and Sybilla firmly closed out the darkness.

"Where's Dylan? Have you seen him?" the singer demanded breathlessly. "Wasn't he marvelous? Wasn't he a *man?*" Sybilla flung out her arms. "*Let's add our seasoned strength* . . ."

But her words were drowned out. In the living room it looked as though a wild game of musical chairs was in progress. Everytime Rosalind and Viola found a seat for someone, somebody else would arrive. Dylan and Mr. Cardiff pushed in the back way.

"Where's Toby?" roared his father.

"Dylan!" shrieked Sybilla.

"Is Toby here?" Mr. Cardiff repeated, raising his voice.

"If you can't see him, you can certainly smell him," Olivia said pertly. "He's been in a stable."

"Over here — behind the piano." Toby, smelling very ripe, tried to wrestle Pistol down from the curtains. Falstaff, his warm engine churning, threaded his way through a forest of feet and dropped softly into Jenny's lap.

"Would someone please tell me what is going on?" demanded Toby's father.

Someone pounded violently on the front door. Viola blew up her hair to see who it was through the glass.

"It's your cousin," she whispered to Jenny. "There's somebody with her."

"Let them in," Mrs. Cardiff said. Miss McNamara, every ruffle trembling with indignation, quivered into their presence, followed serenely by Evan Montmorency.

"Well!" she said. "Someone just tried to blow up the city, and nobody cared about me except Evan." She fastened his arm to hers. "Evan is a gentleman!"

"This will certainly be a boost for my memoirs," he twinkled. Toby rushed over and put out his hand.

"I'm sorry, Evan," he said. "I'm really sorry — for what I thought, and for the things I said —"

The old man took it. "We'll be friends again," he said kindly. "Of course you hurt me, but then you hurt yourself as well, didn't you? Never mind, we'll mend. We'll mend."

"It's been quite a day," Toby admitted. He sat down on the piano bench. "After I talked with Jenny this morning I was convinced Humphrey had to be the troublemaker, and I made up my mind to do something about it. So I followed him. Except today he delivered milk in that antique wagon, and I followed his horse for miles. I'll never look another tub of cottage cheese in the eye again."

"Why did you follow him?" Mrs. Cardiff asked. "That was so foolish, Toby."

"I wanted to walk up and say, 'You're the one' — but like Hamlet I just kept putting it off."

"Then what happened?" said Rosalind.

"He must have noticed me trailing after him, because he stopped the wagon and asked me what I wanted."

Everyone waited for more.

"So I said, 'Are you the one who has been bothering my family this summer?' hoping he'd say he wasn't so I could forget the whole business and go home. But he just looked relieved and admitted that he was. I think he was tired of being a nuisance."

Dr. McNamara drew smoke down the wrong way.

"I felt silly," Toby went on. "I really wanted to punch him right in the nose, but he was so polite and cooperative that I just couldn't. So I suggested that we go and talk it over with the police. He said he'd *like* to do that, but first he wanted to finish his deliveries, and then he wanted to give me back the cats. He was very sorry he'd taken them — particularly Pistol. He said they were out in the stable where the horse was kept, and that he'd meet me there after dinner."

"You believed him?" Alex Cardiff said incredulously.

"I told him I had to be at the theatre later, but he was stubborn about it. He said he'd make a confession after he'd given me the cats if I didn't talk to anyone first."

"Toby!" his mother said. "What if you'd been hurt?"

"Once I knew who he was I just wasn't afraid any more," Toby explained. "And he did show up, just like he said he would. He wanted to talk about himself. He said that ever since the Festival started nothing seemed to go right for him. He had gotten a job as a stagehand but the manager fired him before the season was over. All his inventions had been failures. He wanted to blame someone or something for his troubles. When Dad let him go last year he just took it out on us. Then he thought of making trouble for the theatre. He told me about starting the fire in the washroom and about the day he heaved a bucket of paint over the figure in Exhibition Hall." Toby cocked an eyebrow at Cousin Cleo. "He said that was Miss McNamara's fault — he'd really wanted to heave a bucket of paint over *her*."

Jenny smothered a laugh.

"Anyway," Toby said, "he gave me the cats, and we'd started back into town when he said, 'I think I've made a big mistake.' I asked him what that was. 'I may have set the bomb all wrong,' he told me. 'It may go off a lot sooner than I planned.' "

"That was the first you knew about the bomb?" Dr. McNamara put in.

"I took off like a Keystone Cop in the movies," Toby said. "I didn't know then that the bomb was harmless — just another one of Humphrey's failures."

"But he couldn't have destroyed the Festival Theatre," Viola said. "One of the strongest things in the world is an idea that works. The Festival would have gone on, and the theatre would have been rebuilt. Didn't Humphrey know that?"

Nobody could answer for Humphrey. Portia answered for herself.

"Hungry," she said.

"And I think it's time for a party," Mrs. Cardiff announced gaily.

"We'll toast Jenny's impromptu debut tonight."

"You'll be in trouble over that," Alex Cardiff warned his son. "But maybe under the circumstances they won't be too hard on you. I think Jenny did a fine job for an instant understudy."

Sarah waved a telegram. "It's from my parents," she said. "It's been raining in New York for over a week. The water shortage is over, and they want me to come home and take a bath."

Laughter was uncorked, like wine foaming from a bottle. It was a rare and lovely moment. Jenny stood by the window and wondered if someday she would be back on the stage of the Festival Theatre. What was it the Chorus had said?

> *"Thus far, with rough and all-unable pen*
> *Our bending author hath pursu'd the story*
> *In little room confining mighty men . . ."*

Mighty men, indeed! Not just kings and courtiers waltzing with destiny — but the players! It was the players who breathed such lusty wind into old sails; who polished all the aged and familiar lines and set them gleaming. To belong to such a cry of players would be high ambition!

Toby came to stand behind her, and they stared up into the vaulting mystery of night. The Festival Theatre at last was safe. And so, at last, was the summer in Stratford. High overhead the bright and busy stars wove an endless glittering tapestry over the city.